LADY BEWARE

I stiffened, trying to identify the sound, but all I could hear was the muffled thump of my own heart. Again—it came again, the swish of a foot on carpet. I raised up on an elbow and stared in strange fascination at the door. Slowly the knob moved. Swiftly I got out of bed and crossed the room to the door and pressed my ear to the panel. There was the faint sound of a departing footfall, the rustle of garments as if the would-be intruder wore long skirts. Then silence. I returned to the bed, but not to sleep. . . .

Diamond Books by Muriel Newsome

THE SECRETS OF MONTROTH HOUSE
CURSE OF THE MOORS
WATCHFUL EYES

WATCHFUL EYES

MURIEL NEWSOME

DIAMOND BOOKS, NEW YORK

This book is a Diamond original edition,
and has never been previously published.

WATCHFUL EYES

A Diamond Book / published by arrangement with
the author

PRINTING HISTORY
Diamond edition / February 1993

ISBN: 1-55773-859-9

Diamond Books are published by The Berkley Publishing Group,
200 Madison Avenue, New York, New York 10016.
The name "DIAMOND" and its logo are trademarks
belonging to Charter Communications, Inc.

PRINTED IN THE UNITED STATES OF AMERICA

10 9 8 7 6 5 4 3 2 1

For Sherrie, Laura, and Belle

CHAPTER 1

❧

I looked down the long, tree-shaded avenue and knew something was there, waiting for me. I had no knowledge of what it might be. I only knew I didn't want to go there, not yet.

I was sitting on a park bench and watching children at play, their shouts all in French, for this was Montreal's French Quarter. For a time I had even followed their games—anything to keep myself occupied for a little longer, putting off what I knew, in the end, I must do.

Three days ago I'd purchased a traveling case, a hatbox, and a new reticule and set out for Canada, thrilled to be invited for a visit to Montreal by Andrea, a friend from school days. A room at a hotel had been engaged and I was to meet her there, but a note that explained her absence had been left at the desk for me. Somewhat frantic, possibly penned in haste, it begged forgiveness; her mother was critically ill and she'd had to leave suddenly for England. She would write as soon as possible. I was disappointed of course but felt deep sympathy and only hoped the situation wasn't as bad as it sounded.

As long as I was here, I'd reasoned, why didn't I get about a bit, see some of the sights, before returning home to Lowelton? It was 1912 and more and more these days, women were taking such excursions by themselves.

I'd enjoyed every minute of my trip so far, and I was certain the decision made that night was correct.

I had always wanted to see Canada, colorful Montreal in particular. I felt free and relaxed. This morning I'd even risen early, already filled with plans for the day.

Then it had happened. All too soon there had been the pull, the strongest inclination to turn down a certain street. I'd resisted, up to a point. I hadn't turned down that street. But it was there waiting; it could wait. So the whole miserable business was starting over again.

I stood up, looking down the long, grass-bordered avenue again, and mentally set my heels. It was past midday but I could still have coffee and, if I wished, something to go with it. Most small bakeshops in the area had tiny lunchrooms where one might be served fresh pastry, together with steaming cups of coffee or tea. I walked to a corner *boulangerie* that resembled nothing so much as a fussy little old lady. Scalloped, multicolored trim adorned every eave, and completely surrounded each of the two front windows, whose ample windowboxes spilled over with brightly colored geraniums.

At the door I met another customer, a big man who wore no hat on his blond head and carried a briefcase under one arm. He stepped aside courteously.

"Thank you," I murmured and moved through the door he held open for me.

Inside, frail wrought-iron chairs and tables of delicate pink and white were clustered behind lace-curtained windows whose sills groaned with knickknacks and potted plants. There were four tables and two of them were occupied. I took one of those remaining while the blond man seated himself at the end of the counter.

He seems curious, I thought as I looked up and caught him looking at me in the large mirror over the coffee bar. He was scrutinizing me intently and for a moment I wondered if he took me for a traveler. It could show even without a map in my hand.

He appeared the solid sort himself, possibly in banking or some allied profession. Large, well-kept, smooth in a strong masculine way. His hair gleamed pale in the overhead light of the corner where he sat. Again feeling his gaze I averted my head, my hat brim covering my rising annoyance. There was no need to be rude if it was my looks he found curious. I knew all too well what I looked like, tall, black-haired, with oddly slanted eyes.

With the remainder of my cruller wrapped and tucked into a pocket, I left before he did, making it a point not to glance his way again.

My blue traveling suit with its white shirtwaist, full walking skirt, and matching jacket seemed almost too warm for this balmy late April day. It was good to walk and breathe the fresh bright air, good to be alive. What would it be like to have a companion to share a day like this, or better still, all the tomorrows to come? But for me that would never happen.

After a stormy childhood I had learned the less people knew about Paulette Kirkwood the better. I was perfectly normal save for the "gift," which had never brought anything but sorrow and trouble. I had learned that there were those to whom the gift of second sight was a blessing. Increasingly this so-called gift was becoming known and publicized. There were even those who for scientific purposes allowed themselves to be examined and tested, but I was not one of them.

There was at least one like me in every generation of my family. My father, grandmother, great-grandfather, and others far back had each borne his or her tragedy. My great-great-grandfather had fled his home because people said he was afflicted with witches. He was locked up but he wasn't mad, it was only that he saw things not of this world and hadn't the sense to keep quiet about it.

I wondered if his wife brought about the incarceration, as my own mother had threatened to do with my father. Of the four children born to them I alone survived, a fact she frequently alluded to as though he were to blame for this, also. That he was able to see and foretell events, always to the common good, to locate with unerring accuracy lost people, lost pets, lost objects, meant nothing to her. He was "odd" and Mother still tapped her head and eyed him askance after years of marriage. I remembered the continual uproar at home, and Mother's ultimate threat of divorce. It was then that my father, a mild and gentle man, put the subject aside completely. He would, he said quietly, help no one anymore, ever; and never, from that day forward as long as he lived, was he heard to mention anything relative to the paranormal.

My own life followed the pattern. Five, and playing hide-and-seek. I'd done as the others did but I'd found my playmates, every one, because I knew exactly where they were hiding. They accused me of cheating and I'd run home in a storm of tears.

Twelve, and the boy lost in the pond. Grandfather, with whom I lived after Mother died, maintained that "the sight" was a precious bestowal and should be cherished, but after what happened to Davey Crenshaw, Grandfather wasn't so sure, either.

In a dream, I knew what was going to happen and said as much to Grandfather. He made a hazardous trip through the snow to warn the boy and his father. Four days later Davey came up missing. At school, panic-stricken, I'd tried to tell my teachers where he was but none of them believed me. Even Davey's parents refused to believe; their son wouldn't be so stupid, Mr. Crenshaw shouted angrily. Almost in hysterics, I'd finally made them listen and led the way to the pond. Davey was *there,* I insisted, he'd gone through the ice and drowned. They found his body there.

I was taken home and put to bed and the doctor called. He prescribed complete rest. The doctor looked at me curiously as he left, however, as if I were a pariah, an outcast from the human race.

It didn't always happen that way, of course. There could be days, weeks, before I'd "know" something again. Sometimes it came as a gentle awareness, at other times it came bursting upon the senses like a thunderbolt, an assault that defied doubt and demanded immediate action. Davey's was like that.

Then in high school came the incident that finally wrote

finish to something eager and young in me. I met a boy. Albert—Albert St. Denis. From the start I thought he was different, and young as I was, I fell in love, utterly and completely. It didn't occur to me to be cautious, that the old stumbling block of my "gift" might stand in the way. One day there was to be a rally and, afterward, a debate with partners. Albert was my partner and I overheard him say, "She's got funny eyes—they look right through you. I don't know how I got paired off anyhow—old Rivet-Eyes got me in a corner, I guess. No, I don't know whether her grandad's crazy or not, but they say he sees things." Every dream I'd ever had came crashing down. I turned quietly and went home, to lock myself in my own private world of misery.

Grandfather comforted me by saying that second sight was still precious and to be cherished but that people just didn't understand. Better not to say anything.

Having grown a great deal wiser by this time, I agreed with the last, but not with Grandfather's advice that I get out more, make friends, have fun. He sold the farm and we moved into town, but it didn't do much good. I knew my grandfather was disappointed in me until the day he died. I was nineteen then, out of school and with a year and a half of Academy behind me. I went to work in the library and it was there I met Andrea and we became friends. Somehow I managed to hide my oddness from her. I never saw Albert St. Denis again. Silently I now sent up a plea to the blue sky; with such a past, what could the future possibly hold?

All at once I paused and looked around, uncomfortably aware how far my steps had taken me. I was in unfamiliar territory and for a moment was deeply frightened. The street was winding and narrow, the old unkempt buildings drab and crowded shoulder to shoulder with their tops leaning so far over the cobbled roadway they appeared about to collapse upon the unwary passerby.

There were no street markers anywhere and nothing at all to tell me where I was. The feeling of disorientation grew; the walls were closing in, they were going to crush me, any moment now they would topple and I would go down beneath them, earth to earth under dust and rubble. I shuddered, a paroxysm of deep, dredging cold, and knew I had no wish to venture further, no desire to penetrate that darkening alley. There was nothing here for me and I had to get back to the sunshine, to the pure golden light of day. I turned to flee but it was as though I stood in deep waters and could not move. Waters swirled around me; my limbs had no volition of their own and no strength.

The skies too had grown suddenly dark, the mists were closing in. My frightened eyes glimpsed gaunt white faces peering from the gaping windows and cold crept deeper inside my clothes, clammy against my skin.

On the chill wind came the strong odor of dankness and decay, of human excrement, of slop, and nearby, I heard the snuffle of animals rooting in the street. The air was rank with garbage, and filth flowed in a central channel. There was a splash as some avid, furry creature slithered off into the darkness and I suppressed a scream. I reeled back in horror and threw up protecting arms as a dray thundered past and disappeared into the distance. I could hear the thudding echo of the horses' hooves as they grew fainter, then died away altogether. Voices came out of the gloom, a great clatter and raucous laughter. Snarling dogs snapped at a pile of offal almost at my feet.

There was a signpost—this place had a name, Limpole Road. I could barely see through the clotted shadows; shreds of these shadows swirled before my eyes. Then something forced my gaze up, up, and there, above me, high above and towering over the dark, mean street, was the House.

Why, I thought, I have been here before! I know this place. I know it! How can this be? Yet I recognize it—

In this moment there was a vacuum; no birds, no air, no universe, everything sucked dry of life and motion, time and space stood still. There was only this huge animate Thing upon a hill, the house that had owned me and now had found me again.

I stood rooted to the spot and stared up at it. Huge, sprawling, many dormered, many windowed, blue, painted all blue, even the roof. The windows were the only spots of bright color. They caught that color from the afternoon sun.

The house was no stranger to me. This I knew, this was the knowledge I had in my mind, in my consciousness, since—when was it? I could not have said. There it stood, immense, imposing, as though it had settled itself an eon ago just to enjoy the view, then deciding to stay, haughtily assumed its royal prerogative to govern all it surveyed. A château, now blue, now modern perhaps, certainly with people in it I did not know. But the house I knew, there was no strangeness to that. I had been here before in whatever life I had lived then, and it knew me.

The mists were receding, the waters receding, the power that arrested me and snapped my strength fading away. Again the sky was blue; chittering swallows swooped and dived among the chimney pots. The air was clean and fine and glistening and there was no more smell of excrement, of dank earth and rotting garbage; it was all gone, wagons and horses were gone, all of it silently vanished back into that age from which it had come.

I searched the row of buildings and the street and found the scene once more exactly as it should be, old structures leaning, tired, dusty, venerable, nothing more than a picturesque alley. *Limpole Road.* I would never find it again for in this day and time it did not exist.

I faced forward and slowly began to climb the hill.

CHAPTER 2

❧

This street paralleled the broad, tree-shaded upper avenue where the mansion was located. It was a roundabout route. Five blocks farther on and after a turn to the left and a long, gradual climb I halted at last to stand before the vast structure which had drawn me. From this distance, it looked different.

A gracefully curving driveway led up to a wide porte cochere obviously under repair. The front entryway as well as a section at the corner of the house was being rebuilt, but the main building, huge and blue, with its ornate porches and many old-fashioned dormer windows on the west side, were as I had seen them from below. The feeling of antiquity was very strong. The numbing terror that had gripped me earlier was gone but the sense of the inevitable remained, as did recognition, and the certainty that I was, in some strange way, bound to the house.

Then I saw the sign in the window, Dinners Served, and knew the château to be some sort of lodging house, or inn. Apartments or suites of rooms, perhaps? I moved up the long front walk bordered by daffodils and mounted the broad steps, then paused—or did one simply stride in as though he had the right to do so? Hesitantly I lifted the great brass knocker, let it fall, and waited. Nothing happened. Before I could lift the knocker again the heavy door opened and an austere personage stood before me.

"Yes?" The woman's demeanor was forbidding but her words were courteous enough. "What is it?"

I felt like shoving my serviceable reticule farther behind me and out of sight. Instead I clutched the strap more firmly and indicated the sign. "I could have come right in," I said, "but I wasn't sure of the procedure. Is this a public house? Are you—that is, your services are not only for your regular customers, are they?" To my discomfiture I realized I was stammering. Then I straightened. "You do serve meals?" I asked in a more normal voice.

"Yes," she said briefly. She wore a long skirt of some striped material and a stiffly starched, high-collared gray shirtwaist, her sparse hair drawn into a severe bun atop her head. Her face was long and sallow and the dark eyes showed no warmth at all. "The dining room opens at four o'clock," she pronounced. "Madame Crecy insists upon accommodating her hours to suit the convenience of her tenants, most of whom are elderly and wish to retire at an early hour of the evening. It is not yet four o'clock. Or are you selling something?"

I felt my jaws tighten sharply. "No, I am not selling anything."

"Very well." The woman moved aside. "Come in. I am Mrs. Divino, the *directrice*. A waitress will show you to a table. Coffee only, or tea. We do not serve before the appointed hour."

"Tea will be fine," I said stiffly.

"Tell the girl, not me." The woman swung back, frankly looking me up and down, then lingering on my face with a gaze turned suddenly sharp. "Do I know you? I have seen you somewhere. Have you been here before?" I shook my head but when I would have replied I was cut off. "No. I must be mistaken."

The house didn't fall down upon me; I felt no creeping menace or clawing fingers as I stepped over the threshhold and into the deep soft rug. I was conscious only of extreme beauty and the perfumed warmth all about me. The surroundings were also very French. Eighteenth-century tapestries covered the walls of the large entryway that opened into an immense dining area already half filled with early comers. Every head in the room turned, most either bald or bearing crowns of snow-white hair.

The *directrice* gestured and moved away and a bright-eyed girl in a frilly white cap and apron appeared. "Mademoiselle?" There was a quick curtsy and a smile. "Will you follow?" She led the way and saw me seated. I began to feel a warm glow. Here was charm and welcome and a delightful French accent all rolled into one. "Tea? Is very nice."

"Please," I said gratefully. "With milk. No lemon."

"*Très bien*. I bring at once."

After the initial chill, warmth was most soothing. I looked around, now free to admire the vast room and observe the diners with heads bent over well-appointed tables. There was the gleam of linen and silver and crystal, with a fresh hothouse rose in a sparkling cut-glass vase at each place setting. After some initial moments of curiosity the elderly ones accepted my presence and again addressed themselves to their teacups. An air of elegance lay over everything, as gentle as the diffused rays shed by the chandeliers.

I'd started the day with the distinct reminder that I was not mistress of my own destiny, that once again I was being led by that dark force that governed my existence. But there was no evidence of darkness here, no slightest hint of anything fearful or intimidating. When the waitress came I asked, "Do you have apartments to let?"

"To let? *Oui*. I believe so, if there is room." The girl smiled.

"By the night?" It was impulse only, a notion which, if gratified, could put a dent in my finances, yet might be well worthwhile.

The girl hesitated. "I think not the overnight guests. But about this I am not sure, Mademoiselle. Perhaps it is best to ask the *directrice*. I will inquire for you. One moment, please."

Turning to look, I was startled to see that the blond man, the one I'd encountered earlier in the doorway of the café, was entering the dining room. The manager was nowhere to be seen; she had obviously gone off about her own duties, and the little waitress was speaking to the man as if she knew him. She nodded toward me, he acknowledged her question, then he threaded a path through the diners to come directly to my table. For a shocked moment I'd wondered if he followed me here, then discarded the idea as foolish.

"Good afternoon." He inclined his head pleasantly. "We met at the bakery, if you remember? I'm early too and it seems we have a habit of winding up in the same place at the same time. I notice you appear to be new at the Château and I wanted to extend a welcome."

I was surprised and more than a little taken aback—wary too, at the suddenness of his attention, but he certainly seemed sincere. I could only accept the welcome in the spirit in which it was being offered. "Why, that is kind of you, Mr. . . . ?"

"Jason Nettleton, with the firm of Peters and Nettleton. I am Madame Crecy's solicitor and a regular at Crecy House. As a matter of fact I spend a good share of my free time here."

So he was very much connected with this place! "I . . . see," I murmured. What could I say? He was still standing. "Would you care to sit down, Mr. Nettleton?"

"Thank you. I would." He gave a slight bow and seated himself. A man, I judged, who took problems in stride and attacked obstacles head-on. He was not handsome, especially upon closer inspection, but compelling; square-faced, with a heavy mouth and chin, he radiated strength and determination. Should one cross him, he would be a formidable foe.

There was a pause as coffee was brought for him. I took a sip of my tea and glanced up, interrupting a particularly searching gaze. He smiled at once to cover it. "Well, what do you think of the château? I saw you evaluating it as I came in."

Evaluating was an odd word but I answered without reservation. "I think," I said slowly, "this surely is the most beautiful house in the world. I have never seen anything like it. Outstanding! Is it very old?"

"Parts of it, yes. It is one of the few remaining show-pieces in the area, and of inestimable value. This one has had good care, everything lavished upon it that money could buy. It's an antique and antiques go to pieces very rapidly unless you keep them up. Rebuilding will begin on the Old Wing shortly. Materials are a bit hard to come by right now because of the labor unrest—you may have heard about it—but Madame has a crew coming the first of the month."

"Well worth rehabilitating," I remarked, adding that I'd noted some construction going on at the front of the house.

Above the dining room on the far side there was a long curved balcony in the French style. The waist-high balustrade was made of intricate metal grillwork and the balusters were each adorned with a bust or marble statuary. Did these represent the ancestors of the Crecy people?

The balcony was where the musicians of long ago would have gathered to serenade the diners below, or to play for the dancing crowd. Sweetly the strains of a lovely minuet drifted downward to swirl about us. I tipped my head, startled. Couldn't Mr. Nettleton hear? Instinctively I glanced around; no one else had heard it, either. No shocked old eyes were raised to the source of that sound; there were no lulls in the pleasant muted murmur of well-bred conversation. The balcony was empty. No musicians sat there; there were no instruments—there was no music. I had imagined it all.

"Is there something wrong?" Jason Nettleton asked, but I shook my head.

"No. Really. Just appreciating."

"You like this sort of thing."

"I do, indeed."

He pointed upward and I suppressed a gasp. The domed ceiling above us was an artist's dream. Presented in life-sized paintings of incredible beauty and brilliance were figures both in repose and in motion, each section depicting some different facet of court life.

"Wonderful. A masterpiece," I murmured.

"True," he agreed. "This ceiling dates from the middle seventeen hundreds, the balcony baluster, the early six-teenth century."

I'd felt the place had history, but this was fascinating. "It has to be European. How did the ceiling get here?"

"It was dismantled of course, and brought over on shipboard from France."

"The original owner of Crecy bought it?"

"No, not precisely. It was intended for the mansion of a nobleman, but Thomas of Crecy was the better gambler and the prized dome wound up in his possession and was carted off to the New World."

"This Thomas was something of an adventurer, I take it."

"According to all accounts, he was that. A colorful character, to be sure. The old swashbuckler brought back something else, too—a native girl from the Pacific Islands. Quite a blow to the family, so the story goes, but even that failed to ostracize him."

"You seem to know a great deal about this house," I commented when Jason Nettleton paused. He shrugged with a wry grin.

"Actually, I like the old place. But forgive me. I can hear myself and the way I've run on."

"Oh no," I said quickly, "not at all." My initial stiffness had worn off completely and I was engrossed. "Do continue with what you were saying. Did this fabled Thomas marry the girl?"

"Yes, and thrust her upon society, too. There is evidence of his travels all over the house—bric-a-brac, ivory, carved teak, and jade. He was a fancier of that sort of thing. It is said he supplied the French throne with many of its finest pieces. A collection of miniature dolls, with some fiendishly clever caricatures, is still intact."

"It is here in this country?"

"In this house. King Louis coveted the collection but Thomas wouldn't hear of it. My idea is that Thomas enjoyed tantalizing him. There is a Grand Ballroom; history says they had some lively entertainment there when it was part of the main house. Crecy was a showplace even then and everybody who was anybody flocked here. It's well known that Louis himself contemplated a trip to view its wonders but changed his mind.''

''I wonder why?'' I said. ''Weren't conditions in France quite bad at the time? I believe I remember that part of my French history quite well. As it was, I'm surprised he considered coming at all.''

''His homeland,'' Jason Nettleton chuckled, ''or the royal neck? With the wilderness howling at Crecy's back door, so to speak, he may have felt it was safer where he was than in Little France, as this part of the country was then known.''

''So much from the past,'' I mused, ''so much all in one man and his descendants.'' I wondered how it would be to live in such a place, with cherubim gamboling on the ceiling; to tread its halls and to steep myself in its beauty. Even the fact that the Château was now a hotel, virtually a rooming house run for old people, didn't detract from its appeal. ''How long have you been the Crecy solicitor?'' I asked.

''A little better than three years. I was originally from Maine, just getting started here, and Madame gave me a hand. I've flourished ever since.'' His smile was broad and disarming as he leaned forward across the table. ''All this talk and I don't know anything about you.''

I told him my name and where I was from, beyond that adding only that I'd been but a short time in Montreal and would soon be going back.

''Then this is your first day?''

''The second. I spent last night at a hotel.''

''You should have come here first.''

''That would have been nice,'' I replied evasively. Three years, he'd said, so he was probably in his middle thirties now, with an assurance that would carry him across any threshold. A little too forward for my taste, but interesting, and I shared his enthusiasm for the Château.

''If you care to, you could stay. I'm sure the house has ample accommodations.''

''But—'' I shook my head. ''Do they rent rooms by the day?''

"I don't see why not. I don't foresee any problem at all. The girl spoke to me about it so I already knew what you had in mind. If you want a room you may have one."

"I'd like that," I said. So he had a great deal of influence here, too. Well, I was not surprised. I followed his gaze to that upper balcony, catching a brief movement as someone withdrew, someone who had been looking down upon the diners. It was a glimpse only; perhaps it had been a servant going about her duties, I thought.

At the far end of the dining room a stairway rose to meet the balcony. Close beside the steps was what, from here, appeared to be some sort of ramp. Innumerable doors opened off the corridor. "What is up there?"

"Madame's quarters, some apartments, then farther on back, more apartments, most of them unoccupied on that floor. Would you like to meet the Mistress of the Château?"

"Oh, I hardly think so!" I was taken completely off guard. "I doubt she would appreciate a stranger coming in upon her."

He laughed. "Not a stranger, a guest. And you would be surprised how resilient she is." He pulled a heavy gold watch from a vest pocket and glanced at it. "Do come, Miss Kirkwood. It's quite all right, and we still have time before dinner."

"If you're sure—" I murmured. But why not? The meeting would surely be interesting, something to be remembered.

We skirted the dining room to the accompaniment of interested stares and mounted the steps to the landing, where, I saw, the ramp also ended. I was curious as to the purpose of such an arrangement but before I could ask, my companion spoke.

"There is a saying in this house that around every corner is a view. That may not be entirely accurate but there is a particularly pleasant one just down the hall a few steps." He pointed. "If you would like to see?"

Again I hesitated, then nodded. I might as well make the most of the time I was here. He took my arm and guided me

the short distance down the carpeted passageway to halt
midway past a long row of oriel windows.

"What do you think of that?"

Below, a whole miniature world lay before us, with
emerald-green lawns broken by clumps of primroses and
tulips nodding in the late-day sun, the sparkle of pool and
fountain, and through the shrubbery, the vague outline of a
small structure whose roof was painted blue.

"A summerhouse," he explained. "That's the corner of
it, the rest is behind that clump of greenery. The cobblestone
path leads from the house—a separate entrance. Roses are in
season. Madame has some of the finest rose beds in the
country."

"Superb," I breathed. "A little hideaway. A jewel."

"Not so little," Jason Nettleton replied. "This is only
part of it. The rest continues along the side of the house out
of sight. Even the walls of the house are screened by trees;
there are picnic tables, benches, and chairs. Clever plantings
only make the garden look small and intimate. Secluded."

"Whoever did the landscaping must be a master at his
craft," I marveled. "It all looks so natural, exactly as if it
grew that way."

"That's the way it's supposed to look. Built for her
tenants—with their shawls, canes, and carpet slippers.
Everything that money can buy." There was a distinct edge
to his voice. "Never spare the dollars if it gives them what
they want."

Did that mean he was not in accord with the way the
money was spent? I was somewhat shocked but it was not
my place to comment. "Apparently," I observed lightly,
"this Château is Madame Crecy's pride and joy. I can't
think of a more worthwhile project to lavish money upon, so
long as one has the money."

"Of course," Jason Nettleton agreed, his heartiness
returning. "Well put! And she's very fond of her people.
All you have to do is look around to see that. Naturally she
has her own private garden too, a little smaller than this one,
but fully as striking." He went on to explain that the
balcony we'd passed, the one overlooking the dining room,

was a relic from earlier days and her favorite observation point. She often appeared there to chat and wave down to her "guests," as she referred to them.

My gaze returned to the window, and I lost myself again in the vista below. Sunset glowed on the summerhouse roof and turned it to sapphire and the fountain scattered golden droplets. If Madame's retreat was half as lovely as this one, it must be beautiful indeed.

But a change had come almost imperceptibly, as if a cloud had passed over the sun, or as if a breeze had drifted through the hallway disturbing the air currents. It was behind me—no, all around me. *This place is full of them*, my thoughts said. Spirits. I might have known! I can feel them, like—like the girl standing in the alcove over there. Not nebulous but fully formed and wholly visible. The girl suddenly smiled, a saucy, impish grin, and only then did I note the long ruffled skirts, the tight-laced velvet bodice, the black curls tumbling in wild abandon to the shoulders. *But I saw my own face!* Peace and hope quavered, died miserably. Was I losing my mind? I'd looked at myself and myself looked back at me. Yet the apparition was dressed in clothes of another time.

The garden had lost its color; I was seeing it through a veil of frustrated tears. When I looked back the girl was gone.

Mr. Nettleton hadn't seen, of course, nor been aware of anything out of the ordinary. "How do you like it?" he wanted to know.

"Wonderful," I said, and struggled hard for calmness. "Thank you for showing me. But," I added as we retraced our steps down the hall, "I'm having second thoughts. I'm not at all certain it's a good idea to visit the Mistress of Crecy unannounced."

"No," he assured me, "it's perfectly all right. Beyond that door is her suite of rooms."

"Is she—formidable?" For I suddenly and most definitely wished I hadn't come.

"Very," he agreed gravely. "Eighty-two, a will of iron, and famed for her forceful opinions, pungently expressed."

An eyebrow quirked. "Not dangerous or given to attack, except verbally."

Perhaps I should not be so reluctant, but it had occurred to me that I'd agreed too readily. To force myself upon anyone, especially the mistress of this beautiful old creation perched upon its own hill, was not my way. Why hadn't I refused at once and stuck with it? "If you're trying to put me at ease, you're not succeeding," I asserted. "She'll think I'm impossible and cheeky, and she'd be right. Why, I'm not one of her tenants." There was no reply, nor had I expected one.

Spaced at regular intervals down the ramp I'd noted before were small protuberances, obviously nailed or secured to the boards beneath.

"Chocks," Jason explained, "safety measures for her wheelchair in case the chair gets out of hand, to slow it down or to stop it. Three-cornered pieces of wood, most of which are covered with carpet, to act as an emergency braking system. See?" He indicated with his foot. "She is by no means the recluse one might think—the house is honeycombed with ramps. An excellent way to get from one floor to another."

Wheelchair, I thought. Eighty-two? I knew I should not have come. But there was no turning back now. As Jason raised his hand to knock, the door opened abruptly and the gaunt dark woman, Divino, stood before us blocking our path.

"Oh. It's you." Her eyes flicked over me, dismissing me, and returned to Jason. "Madame's not seeing anybody."

"She'll see me," Mr. Nettleton suggested. "And Miss Kirkwood is with me. Mrs. Divino," he announced, as if suddenly remembering his manners, "but undoubtedly you have already met." An irony not lost on me.

"You are not expected." It was a statement, not a question, and he countered with equal brevity.

"Let us pass, if you please."

Mrs. Divino stood like a bulwark guarding her mistress's door and I couldn't blame her for that. Eyes black and deep set in the pale face, both face and bearing suggesting a rigid self-control, she was a figure to command respect. But there was something else, only vaguely sensed before, that puzzled yet repulsed me, and my hackles unexpectedly rose. It was something inside the woman's skin, that lived with her and was a part of her.

"I tell you Madame's orders were that she was not to be disturbed."

Jason's question was immediate. "Is she ill?"

"No!"

"Then we will enter."

Divino's eyes shot fire, but she gave ground. Inside, he shut the door carefully. A wheelchair was pulled up before a window, its occupant staring down into a courtyard still bright with late day.

"Don't pussyfoot. I heard you coming. And saw you from the balcony."

"You saw me from the balcony?"

"You know I did. What's this all about, anyway?" The deep voice vibrated across my nerves. "You don't get away with as much as you think you do."

"You know I keep trying." Jason chuckled and reached for the outstretched hand as the chair swung.

"What, no flowers? Last time you picked my own and gave them to me," the old lady grumbled, "and expected me to like it. You have no news, and heaven knows why I keep you on the payroll. You gallop about the country on one wild-goose-chase after another and come up with nothing. You bully me beyond all bearing—" She caught sight of me and broke off at once. "Who is that?" She'd had her back to the window with the room half in shadow; now she wheeled the chair forward with unexpected vigor and switched on the desk lamp. The old lady's face and figure, abruptly visible in the light, deeply impressed me. A *grande dame* and every inch regal in spite of the sagging flesh of age, the parchment skin, and thin, snowy hair that clung in sparse tendrils to the well-shaped head. Her eyes were clear and searching, her brows heavy, mouth still firm.

"Well—?" Madame Crecy prompted. Suddenly she started as she viewed me more closely, the same shocked

disbelief coming to her as it had to Jason earlier, and her
eyes widened, then she glanced at Jason. What was wrong
with everyone in this house? Caught between these two
people and understanding neither of them, I felt obliged to
say something.

"I'm sorry," I murmured stiffly to Madame, "if I've
startled you. I shouldn't have come unannounced. I'll go
now. I should never have come!"

"Never mind that," the old lady muttered. "Your name,
girl? What is your name?"

Jason hastened to make the formal presentation. There
was a pause and Madame Crecy seemed to draw in upon
herself. "Kirkwood, you say, Paulette Kirkwood. I see,"
she said finally. "Do you mind my asking how you got
here?"

I decided to be frank. "I am from Lowelton, in the United
States. I was to have met a friend for a visit but she was
called away unexpectedly by the illness of her mother. She
left for England before I arrived. I'd always been interested
in Montreal and so decided to see some of the sights before
returning home. My wanderings brought me to this house."

"You two have met before? You and Jason?"

"I met her in a café," Jason said, "or rather, I saw her in
the café. We met in the doorway. Then when I saw her here
I introduced myself."

"Makes sense," the old lady said, "so far," but her brow
furrowed. What was she thinking? That there was something strange about my coming? No, that was farfetched,
she couldn't possibly know. "Well," she said on a lighter
note, "it is nice to meet you, Miss Kirkwood. And forgive
an old lady, I didn't mean to sound inhospitable. In
eighty-odd years I have learned to be aggressive. I shall
never unlearn it. A bad habit, I am sure—" She didn't
finish. Instead she stared at me, shook her head wonderingly, and was still. I looked at Jason in mute appeal.

"Ready to go?"

"Oh, but you're not leaving, are you?" Madame Crecy
roused herself to protest. I was glad when Jason insisted
cheerfully. Miss Kirkwood—Paulette—had come for dinner

and dinner she should have. What were they serving tonight?

"Roast duck." The old lady sighed. The urgency seemed suddenly gone out of her; with Jason she was all at once gentle and resigned, as if with a beloved son. "Chestnut sauce. An ice. Ask the cook for anything else you might want—you know."

"All right," Jason agreed. "But one thing more. Would there be rooms to let for the night?"

"I expect so. Why? Is there any question? Miss Kirkwood is staying, of course. Tell Hilda to give her her choice."

"All right," Jason said again. He reached down and gently brushed the old lady's wrinkled brow. "Beautiful," he said.

Her head rested against the chair's back. She measured us both, the eyes deeply veiled as they touched me. "Don't flatter," she said sharply to Jason, "you know I hate flattery." But the reprimand was tempered with humor. "And take care that the girl is treated well."

Jason nodded, but I felt the old lady's piercing stare boring into my back as we left the room.

CHAPTER 3

Away from Madame Crecy, I relaxed. The regular diners observed me for a moment or two when I first entered the dining room, then returned to their food. The dinner was perfect—everything as it should be—the wine exactly the correct temperature, vegetables and fruit crisp and delicious, the "ice" accompanied by tiny orange shortbread that melted in the mouth like golden snowflakes.

"What do you think of Madame Crecy?"

I had been expecting Mr. Nettleton's question. "More to the point," I replied ruefully, "is what she thought of me. I doubt she liked the idea of a stranger popping in on her unannounced. I should have known better."

"Then you didn't like her."

"Why do you say that? I only think she was upset, and it wasn't fair to do that to her. Particularly since she seemed to recognize me. I must look like someone, I've never seen a reaction quite like that before—it was disconcerting, to say the least."

"Yes, she is direct." He reached for a hot roll, carefully buttered it and replaced the knife. "I knew she'd seen me from the balcony and I believed she'd seen you as well, and would want to meet you. That's why I was so insistent. Actually, you're one in a million. In all the time I've known her I have never heard her say she was sorry. Not to anybody. She was unexpectedly gentle tonight."

22

"I can't think why," I murmured. "I gathered that I'd shocked her, and I was ready to leave right then. I will admit, though, that she frightened me just a little. Or perhaps *intimidated* would be a better word. I've never met anyone like her."

He had big even teeth and they glistened when he smiled. Affable, pleasant, and, I noted, very virile. "*Maman* seemed quite taken with you."

I shook my head at once. "Oh no, I'm sure not. Not at all. But she is a very grand lady, and for my part, aside from the consternation my appearance caused, I'm glad I went. Does she have a family?"

"No, she hasn't, and for a Crecy, lineage is all-important. It's almost a phobia with her. What family there was has scattered far and wide, died or generally run out—it wasn't prolific to begin with. And *Maman* is getting old."

"I can't see her running down," I commented gravely. "One can almost feel the tremendous power emanating from her. Having lived to this great age and remaining young and alert is an accomplishment in itself. Does she handle any of her own affairs?"

"Some of them, and all of the household business. She has those well in hand. I'm happy to say I've been able to take a share of the load off her shoulders otherwise."

I took a sip of my coffee, found it cool and drank it anyway. I became aware that he'd leaned his arms on the table and was looking intently at me, a searching gaze that was disturbing.

"We don't get many Americans here, nor, as you can imagine, are there many young faces. It is refreshing and intriguing to see one. Do you mind if I make a personal observation? You have the most most unusual eyes. Large, black, almond-shaped. Almost Oriental. Opaque and un-readable. But I can see I've embarrassed you."

For I'd gone still. Thanks for nothing, I almost said; why had he noticed my eyes? Cat's eyes, Rivet-Eyes—

"Thank you," I managed. "I guess."

"You guess?"

"It's just that I've been teased about them for as long as

I can remember. I am not Polynesian, I am not Balinese, Chinese, or a mix of any of those. All I am is myself.''

He shook his head. "I am most sincerely sorry—I meant nothing disrespectful by my remark. I only meant that your eyes are beautiful. But I was presumptuous—please forgive me?"

After a moment I nodded, regretting the outburst. It was unfair, he couldn't have known. "I should not have spoken out so quickly," I said. "A habit from childhood, I suppose." Yet I was puzzled. Why was he taking such an interest in me? I was no more than a guest, my stay admittedly a brief one. Why had he singled me out? I was not naïve enough to believe that a man assured, attractive, an authority behind the Crecy throne—certainly with a choice of women companions—would be interested in a stranger. He was going to great lengths. Or was it just his way? His profession would require him to meet people, put them at their ease. That must be it, I thought, he was only being kind.

"Do you have any idea what color you want?"

"Color?"

"The decor—" He grinned. "It means a lot in this establishment. Another Crecy hallmark, that the surroundings should suit the occupant. I'm talking about your room. What color would you like?"

"My choice? Now that's silly." But why not go along with the spirit of the thing? "Then lavender, I suppose, or blue, because pansies are my favorite flower."

"Pansies? You surprise me. I'd thought it would be tiger lily, or a combination of red and silver."

I could feel the hot blood rush to my cheeks. He spoke up at once. "I am accustomed to taking the initiative, but I can get carried away. I've embarrassed you again and I'm sorry once more, and I'd better change the subject before I get into deeper water. See that cupola up there, the one with the portrait of Queen Anne hanging below it? It was added in 1732.''

"Seventeen *twenty*-two." I could have bitten my tongue out. Why had I said that? How had I known? Jason was staring at me in astonishment. "It does look eighteenth century," I added lamely. "I know a little about such things, not much. But I've studied some. Mostly about furniture. We had quite a library at home. I love fine old things, don't you? I actually know very little about architecture and that was just a guess." I caught myself; I was babbling. But the maneuver had evidently succeeded for he went on explaining some of the other changes that had come about over the years.

"The Château itself, this part of it, was added in 1701," he said. "It was turned over to the governor, who was to have opened it to Louis the Fifteenth of France when he visited here in 1730. But as I told you, he didn't come; however, his considerable retinue did, and they were lodged and entertained most royally during their stay. The next in line to own it—our roistering sea captain having gone to his reward and his Manona with him—allowed the place to run down badly, leaky roofs, sagging floors. It wasn't until 1790 or around that time that any substantial alterations or repairs were made. It is said the Château had a ghost then, a Simon Medlar, who moved in and made himself at home. An unwelcome guest and a tenacious one, so the story goes, who emptied the ballroom one gala party night. I can just see the ruffle-skirted ladies and becurled and scented gentlemen scrambling over one another to be first to get out the door."

"You do make it sound intriguing!"

"Well, I can hope the tale is true. Don't you? And now what can you see with those black almond eyes of yours?"

"Nothing," I said steadily. "Who was Simon Medlar?"

"Hanged for wife-beating, cow-stealing, husband-killing, and various other diversions, by order of His Grace the Governor, in the square right out there—not fifty feet to the right of the walk you took when you entered the house. Miss Kirkwood—Paulette—is anything the matter?"

"N-no." *It wasn't there at all, it was down nearer where the city is now, perhaps a mile or more. I passed it once and there was a man hanging on the gibbet but his name wasn't Simon Medlar. I ran all the way home and was sick when I arrived. Deborah held the pan for me.* Who, I thought wildly. In heaven's name, who was I then? "I'm—fine."

He was instantly concerned. "You're ill—I'm sorry! Come, let me get you out of here—get some air—" He thought it was something I'd eaten that hadn't agreed with me.

It was a crisis narrowly averted. Would I keep having such visions so long as I remained under this roof? Swift, startling awareness of another self, another time—other surroundings; small, sharp glimpses of a daily life in some world of long ago.

I sat on the edge of the bed with its lavender satin coverlet and looked around the lovely room all lavender and pink and gold; I pressed my hands to my cheeks but the skin was cool, fresh to the touch.

My thoughts kept returning to the girl in the alcove, laughing back at me, the black eyes dancing, the black curls in riotous disarray. In the parlance of the day, a little wanton, I would have said, one of a lower station who could have been tumbled in haymows, whose ripe red lips were any man's for the taking. Myself? The eyes, I thought, but the eyes were deep, sooty, black as night, and mine were dark, but not black. I'd mistaken the apparition for myself because we looked much alike, but we were only alike in some ways. The color of hair, the shape of face, the slant of eyes—these were the same, but it was not me. It was with a sense of relief I realized this, and wondered who it could be then? Some ghost prowling the Crecy halls; my own private ghost that had followed me here? That was no more ridiculous than Simon Medlar, for weren't there many who had seen him?

I went to bed lighter hearted than before and fell asleep almost at once. It must have been near midnight when I woke, startled. There was someone in the room with me, a vague outline limned against the filmy lace curtains; but in the brightest of moonlight and with its back to the window it cast no shadow.

"Who's there?"

The figure advanced to the bed and stood over me. "Yvonne," a small voice said. "I am Yvonne."

I flung back the coverlet and jerked to a sitting position, reaching for the lamp. It was the girl of the alcove, an entity of form and substance which now had voice. With her white frilled waist and black bodice she looked like a picture on a postcard. No, the girl did not totally resemble myself, I saw; it was as I had thought.

She pouted prettily. "I thought you would know. I was sure of it when we met in the hall. Think now. Does not the name Yvonne tell you anything?"

My own name, part of it anyway. I clasped my arms tightly across my breasts to keep from shaking. Of course. Yvonne—there'd been an Yvonne in my family far back— was it my father's great-great-great-grandmother?

The eyes were dancing again, with mischief and with teasing. "I could ha' stirred up a fine storm, could I not? You with your young man. La! but you should have seen me when I was in the world. I kept things merry, I can tell you! Parties, balls, masques—" Her forehead wrinkled and she paused. "I misremember something I came to tell you. No matter, I will think of it by and by."

"Are there others—besides you?"

"Oh, many of us." The girl shrugged, her hands spread in an expressive gesture. "All about, everywhere, though we stay in *la Vieille Maison*—the Old House. This part we do not like, nor do I feel at home here." The small nose wrinkled. "When changes are made, it is never the same. Not many things anymore are as they were in my time. But you are here on this side, therefore I come. I am the bold one, you see. I am always the one to make myself known." She paused again and looked around the room. "It is not like the old days," she repeated sadly, "nothing is the same. Then I did get into much trouble, and caused others to do so." She giggled and once more the black eyes gleamed with mischief. "For that I laughed privily into my pillow at night—aye, I could many times have been forsworn but was never caught. Once even they would have given me the water test—they thought I was a witch—but none would dare; I was of goodly rank and none dared chide me." The black head tipped, studying me carefully. "Do you know my father, you ha' heard of him? The black sheep Joseph de C. everyone talks about. In the China trade. The eyes? I am half Chinese, though I do not look it. You, too, the black eyes and so forth." She added on a plaintive note, "Why must you stay here on this side where we cannot protect you?"

"Protect me from what?" I said sharply.

Yvonne looked at me with pitying eyes. "From evil, my Paulette. It is Evil against Good. There is evil in this house. We are no help over here. We come because you are here but we can do nothing to help you. That you must do for yourself. But you are to have courage, and all will be well."

My throat felt dry. "I don't know of any evil. What kind of evil?"

But she was suddenly restless. She looked around as if disoriented and muttered, "I do not like it over here—if I think to pay you a visit again I will come, yet I think not for long." She put out a hand in a swift, imploring gesture. She seemed to be trying to say something further but then shook her head. And though I was watching, I did not see her leave. One moment the entity was there and the next she was not. I looked at the spot where this girl, this Yvonne, had been, and saw nothing. There was the blank wall, the carpet, the door, and nothing else. I got up and walked across the floor and stood where the girl had stood. Nothing. Yvonne was gone, vanished as though she'd never been.

Now it has become commonplace, I thought, seeing things that aren't there. I held out my hands and studied them; they trembled so violently I put them behind me. I walked stiffly to the dressing table, aware of my jerky, wire-tight movements, and looked in the mirror. Was that white, frozen face my own?

Evil. In this house? What she'd said wasn't true; it was silly. But was it silly when the creature, whatever it was, named herself Yvonne and quoted family history of which I had only the faintest recollection? Joseph de C. I did not know; perhaps I'd heard of him by a different name. The China trade, the rest of it, all had to be true.

She would come back again, she said. I'd forgotten to tell her I wouldn't be here.

CHAPTER 4

After a restless few hours I woke late. I freshened myself,
determined to forget what had happened the night before
and enjoy to the fullest what was at hand. My suite was
majestic—a spacious bathroom, well appointed with extensive conveniences, a large dressing room boasting ample
closet and wardrobes, a sumptuously furnished sitting room
complete with its own view of a section of garden, lawn,
and trees. Everything shining, fresh, bright and beautiful—
truly a beloved house. I'd reveled in the bath, the heavenly
soft towels and scented soap, the delicious warmth, but
having only the one outfit with me—my bags were still back
at the hotel—I had no choice but to put on the same blue suit
as before.

In spite of dressing at a leisurely pace, I descended to the
dining room in time for coffee, which was served with hot
muffins, marmalade, and a message. Would Miss Kirkwood
be kind enough to call upon Madame Crecy, at Miss
Kirkwood's convenience, in Madame Crecy's quarters?

What could the Mistress of Crecy possibly want? It was
not necessary to go, of course. Remembering the upsetting
scene last evening, I decided against it. Some excuse—I'd
have to find some excuse for not honoring the summons.
Madame had given an audience to an unexpected caller
once, and that was enough.

But lingering over the meal I reconsidered. I'd accepted

30

the hospitality of the house, and it would be less than courteous not to listen to what its Mistress had to say. Besides, I confessed to natural curiosity. The visit should only be a pleasant one anyway, now that the initial confrontation was over. Two more days to spend in Montreal—I might even extend my stay to a week, but as lovely and as fascinating as this place was, I'd already made up my mind to spend it elsewhere.

I completed my breakfast then climbed the stairs, noting again the ingenious arrangement of chocks on the ramp. From the ramp's lower landing there was access to the dining room, to other parts of the house, and to the outdoors and the gardens. I paused a moment, looking down. Voices floated in pleasantly from the garden; a serving girl, bearing tray, teapot, and scones, emerged from the direction of the kitchens and turned through the open door. Someone— possibly a group—was having a mid-morning refresher.

I stepped back, returning my attention to the chocks. If one were not careful he could stumble over them very easily, catching a toe on a protuberance to take a bad fall. But the ramps were not for foot-traffic. For a wheelchair, the chocks were indispensable.

I glimpsed Jason down the hall, briefcase in hand, leaving Madame Crecy's quarters. He nodded in greeting and spoke as he came nearer. "Have you had breakfast? I noticed you were down late."

This morning he was dressed in tan trousers and vest to match, he was clean-shaven and looked every inch the professional. Strength and assurance personified, I thought again; he *was* an attractive man. Attractive and interesting.

"Yes," I said. "It was nice, just what I would have wanted. And my suite was wonderful. Since you're obviously on your way somewhere maybe I should say goodbye now, and thank you for your information and your help."

The expression in his eyes was obscure. "Have you seen Madame Crecy yet?"

"No. I was just going there now. She left a message."

An odd look crossed his heavy features, then he suddenly smiled. "I see. Well, I hate to rush off, but I have an appointment. I shall see you at dinnertime." Without waiting for an answer he waved and was gone.

I continued down the hall to Madame Crecy's door. This time there was no forbidding sentinel to impede passage, no dark-browed *directrice* to snarl and growl. I knocked and at once a strong voice called, "Come in, please."

Madame was seated at the desk; she gestured vigorously to a chair. "Do sit down. If you wish the chair up closer you will have to help yourself, as you see, Miss Kirkwood, I am alone." She looked rested and alert, her eyes lively and good color in her cheeks.

"Thank you." I seated myself, looking around. The large room was simply but tastefully furnished, something that I had not taken time to appreciate before. Broad windows with harmonizing curtains, paneled walls hung with a few fine prints, and heavy armchairs, one of leather that was well worn, stamping it as Madame's favorite. There were cabinets and shelves which held journals and ledgers. Beyond the office was an extensive apartment, what appeared to be a bed-sitting room, and a library. On the wall behind the desk was a picture of George V, and nearby, one of the aged Queen Victoria.

"Looks tired, doesn't she?" Madame had followed my gaze. "And sad. They say she never quite recovered from her husband's death." Madame waved a hand. "Do you like the Château?"

"Oh, very much! It's beautiful," I replied with complete honesty. "I know that must have been said many times before, but nothing else fits. I haven't seen much of it but what I have seen is impossible to describe. You must be very proud."

"I am." The old lady was obviously pleased. "It breathes history. The people who walked these halls are long gone but in some way, each has left his mark."

"I can believe that." More than she knew, I thought. I had already made the acquaintance of one of them. "You wanted to see me?" Don't be nervous, I told myself. She's surely not the ogre she seemed before. Hadn't her smile today been warm and welcoming?

"Yes. I thought it might be nice to chat a bit before you left. How long had you planned to stay in Montreal?"

"A few days," I replied, "a week—I'm not sure yet."

The old lady nodded. "Well, you've traveled quite a distance and I am pleased you came. Will your friend be returning? The one you were to have met, whose mother was ill?"

"Oh no," I said, "I'm sure not. Their home was in Devonshire before they moved to Canada and the mother was always homesick. She went back there to live, I think, about a year ago. No, my friend will stay where she was born and grew up."

"Ah, yes. The ties of home are strong."

I wanted to ask if she had ever heard of Limpole Road, but the time hardly seemed appropriate. The question could open a whole series of speculations.

"Did you see Jason?"

"Yes, just as he was leaving."

"I sent a message by him to the contractors; as long as they are at it I want those steps widened. Of course nothing can be done this week—some sort of labor upheaval somewhere—but hopefully they will begin next week. Once they begin, it shouldn't take long to finish. After that, there will be renovation in the Old Wing. Ordinarily this is a quiet place—older people don't like being disturbed and they don't like change. I don't fancy it myself but am of the opinion that if something must be done, get to it. Best get in with repairs before a pillar falls down or a porch collapses."

"Does it upset them?"

"If it does, no one complains. And they're tolerant. It is a nice group here and, I am happy to say, all are congenial. I suppose, in a sense, they've taken the place of family. Do you have a family?"

Why, she wasn't difficult at all, she was easy to talk to, and I felt myself relaxing. "No," I said, "they are all gone, my grandfather was the last. I am alone." Her glance fell to my ringless hands clasped in my lap.

"Then not married."

"No, no sign of it. I am simply a working girl visiting

Canada for a short while.'' I mentioned that after graduation
I had been employed in the Academy library.

"I see." I could feel the old lady's gaze. "I gather there
is French in your ancestry, at least your first name suggests
it. Is there a second name?"

"Yes." I smiled wryly. "Actually, six of them. Paulette
Iona Yvonne Janesse-Poiteau Kirkwood. As a child I
considered writing it P.I.Y.J.P.K."

For a moment there was silence, then she said "I see."
again in a rather distant voice. "Impressive. This could be
decidedly interesting. Have you checked back in your
family tree?"

I shook my head. "Not to any great extent. Great-
grandfather, though, was quite interested in genealogy and
insisted upon the hyphenated Janesse-Poiteau. My grandfather carried it on out of respect. Someone said once that the
Poiteau was supposed to come from some famous general,
but I really don't know." I'd purposely failed to identify
Yvonne, who, along with many of my more immediate
forebears, I would prefer remained buried.

"It is fortunate," she was saying, "that Jason was here
when you came. He is a good talker and knows a great deal.
I imagine he told you something about the place?"

"Quite a bit," I admitted, "and all of it fascinating. I had
no idea such an establishment existed. It is like a city in
itself, it has everything."

"And ghosts."

This was treading on shaky ground. But I could see she'd
meant nothing by the remark, and I answered lightly. "No
doubt plenty of them. This would certainly be the place for
them."

Madame chuckled; she was enjoying this. "Particularly
over in the Old House, what we call the Old Wing. That was
the original structure, or at least part of it. Some of the
smaller sections have been moved over here and incorpo-
rated into this newer portion. If there are those of the
disembodied floating about, I don't mind, do you?"

"Well—I suppose not," I answered, wishing I could

mean it. The recollection of Yvonne's visit—was it only last night?—was still with me.

"You have been very forthright," Madame said abruptly, "I appreciate that. It is not my habit to question but I had my reasons. Would you like to remain, that is, to stay here at Crecy? If you wish, to work for me?"

I was stunned. Here? I found my voice. "Oh, I couldn't possibly! There are reasons—in the first place I am an American citizen. In the second—"

"Arrangements have been made before to cover such situations. It is not uncommon for a citizen of this country to go to the United States, or vice versa, to visit or to remain for an indefinite period of time. I would like you to remain at the Château, as though you were a member of my family."

"But I am not of your family! Besides, this trip was to last only for a short while."

"It could be extended." Madame was totally unmoved by my resistance. "If you accept a long-term offer I would sponsor you. Simply send back word to the Academy."

She meant permanently. I still couldn't believe I'd heard correctly. It was a glimpse into a bright world I'd never dreamed of, and for one brief second, I allowed myself to consider it. Then once again I reminded myself of my problems. I shook my head. "Your offer is extremely generous, but the answer must be no."

"Must be?" Her fine, blue-veined hands rested on the polished arms of the wheelchair, strong, resilient fingers tapping the wood. "You have no one to go back to in the United States, by your own admission no one who needs you. You would not be bound by any agreement here, and would be free to leave any time you chose."

Again I shook my head, wishing there was some way to be tactful yet make it definite. Even if the legal obstacles could be resolved, what about the wraiths that peopled these halls? I had nearly betrayed myself twice when with Jason. There was no reason to suppose such things wouldn't happen again. And what if it got worse? Yvonne said there were others here besides herself. "It's impossible," I said.

"You don't understand—" No, Madame didn't understand, how could she?

Still unconvinced, the old lady continued. "There would be the keeping of ledgers, accounts, possibly even some payroll—I can instruct you in these procedures. I've an extensive doll collection in need of cataloguing. As my personal helper and secretary, you would do whatever is necessary. I assure you it won't be anything complicated; the pay will be good and the hours not long, except when there is paperwork to finish. It is not easy running an establishment this size and I have long considered getting help. I don't want you to do anything you don't want to do, but Miss Kirkwood—Paulette—consider. A most personable and intelligent young lady comes to my home, one with no family, no ties, unmarried, with a rare appreciation of the beautiful and a love for antiques. Can you blame me?"

Her argument wasn't convincing enough. There had to be more to it than that. There must be a dozen, a hundred others who could do as well or better, who would jump at the chance to live in this gorgeous place, but who wouldn't be afflicted by the supposedly unseen and unheard.

"I am a stranger to you," I said. "I still don't understand—why would you do this for me?"

The old lady was silent for a moment. Then she said slowly, "Let's just say you remind me of someone I used to know. Someone very near and dear."

"Is she . . . dead?"

"Dead? Yes, I guess you could say that."

"I'm sorry," I said, "truly sorry," and meant it. "I knew my appearance bothered you but I didn't know why. I never intended to rake up old ashes, please forgive me." I rose and turned to the door. "To say this has been a shock is putting it mildly. I'm pleased that you would consider me, and I don't mean to sound ungrateful, but the answer is still no." I paused with my hand on the knob of the door. "It was kind of you and I'll never forget the offer. I will go home with the memory of this lovely place and what my visit has meant to me."

She said, "You have a week. Why not spend it here?"

I said slowly, "I'm asked to stay in your home, and live on your bounty. Even for a week, call it pride or whatever, I just couldn't do that."

She lifted a hand. "Then if you feel you must make some compensation, there are many ways to help. Your legs are younger than mine and can move about as mine cannot. There would be errands to run, messages to deliver. In the upstairs gallery a portrait is out for restoration; I should like you to keep track of that, and others. There are always such things to be done about the Château. Only a portion of your time would be taken up with these duties, so you can do all the exploring you want. There are so many things to see. In the meantime, do an old lady a kindness and don't make up your mind now. Stay the week, take your time, think it over. If you like Crecy, make it your home." She smiled suddenly, her face lighting up, the smile a little lopsided, a little lonely. I saw, and felt, sympathy. For the first time I felt a rush of warmth for this sturdy old woman. She was trying so hard to give me something I couldn't accept!

"I would be happy to stay the week. That would be . . . wonderful. And thank you," I heard myself say.

"You will? Good! Then you can get about, sightsee. All the newer sections of the Château are open. If you like books, you might visit the libraries; there is a small one here on the second floor and a larger one on the first floor, adjacent to the lounge. You've seen the lounge?"

"Glimpsed it in passing," I assented. "The one off the dining room, you mean."

"Yes. There is also a second gallery, and the Trophy Room. That too is full of history. Ask one of the servants to direct you. And you will want your luggage delivered. Where is it?"

I agreed and told her which hotel. The old lady nodded briskly, and said she would have it sent for at once. I turned to go but she had one more thing to add. "Jason told me he hoped to see you at lunchtime and perhaps show you around a bit afterward but his commitments will keep him all day."

"He doesn't live here, does he?"

"No. He has offices downtown and a suite at the Plado

nearby but he comes to the house often and takes many of his meals here. Says it seems like home to him. His wife died in childbirth and the baby died, too.''

''Oh, what a shame!''

''Yes, it was. A tragic accident. A fine girl from a very wealthy family. Seems she missed her footing and tumbled down a flight of stairs; it brought on premature delivery. He blamed himself for not seeing to greater safety measures, but it couldn't have been anyone's fault. Sometimes I think it was Crecy that brought him out of it. He's very clever, you know, very astute. A bit too preoccupied with money, perhaps, but I suppose that is only natural, since he realized nothing from his marriage. Cleverness and ambition often go hand in hand, and in my case, it has been very helpful.'' She broke off, smiled again. ''Do enjoy the house, and feel free to come visit any time.''

''Thank you,'' I said, ''I will,'' and left.

I almost expected to see ghosts in the hallway; there were none, but an odd smell lingered in the air, like the vague odor of scorch, of something burning or left smoldering. It was like nothing I'd ever smelled before; I couldn't identify it and couldn't locate it, but farther down the passageway I saw the black-garbed figure of the *directrice*. She abruptly halted, then turned to stare directly back at me. The face was hard and cold and without expression, only the eyes burned like hot coals. It was totally unexpected and I stood rooted to the spot. As I watched, the woman faded into a doorway and disappeared. Had she been listening? Posted outside Madame's door to hear all she could hear? What was said couldn't possibly concern her. An uneasy sensation trickled down my spine and I shivered as if icy fingers had touched me.

It was all nonsense of course. I had no dealings with her nor she with me, and I pushed the scene out of my mind. At the head of the steps I was met by one of the upstairs maids; the message delivered was most startling.

''Mademoiselle? There is a gentleman to see you.''

''To see me?'' Not Jason Nettleton, everyone in the

house knew Jason. Besides, he had left some time ago. "Are you sure—did he say he wanted to see *me*?"

"Mademoiselle, but *oui*. I do not mistake. A tall gentleman. *Très beau*." The girl dimpled. "I tell him Miss Kirkwood is with Madame and he must wait." She shrugged. "He wait."

I was even more puzzled. "Didn't he give his name?"

"*Non*, mademoiselle. In the music room at the end of the hall. The gentleman is there."

Who knew of my presence at Crecy? I could not think of anyone who might want to see me. I thanked the maid and went on my way. As I entered the room a stranger rose from a high-backed chair and advanced toward me. *Stranger?* Someone taller than myself, sandy-haired, with a keen, sensitive face and slate-gray eyes—the face and eyes burned into my memory.

Time stopped, breathing stopped, every drop of blood in my body stood still. Then shock pounded through me. I stared at him, numb.

"Albert? Albert St. Denis?" My lips were stiff.

"Paulette? It's been a long time." The same voice, stronger, deeper, a man's voice. He reached out but didn't touch me. Through the numbness I heard him say, "There was a school reunion and you weren't there. Miss Davis—she's still Miss—asked about you. I told her I was coming to Montreal on business and, if possible, would look you up. The Academy knew that your friend Andrea lived here, and you'd taken a leave of absence from the library to visit. I didn't do so well at first but then a waitress in a bakery remembered you but had no idea where you'd gone after leaving there. I made a guess, and here I am."

Yes, I thought, here you are. A man, a stranger, stood before me, yet still so much the boy I knew, had dreamed about and agonized over for so long. And remembering, all the old torture came back and I was deeply, crushingly hurt. That he would hunt me down like this—

"Why are you here?"

A quieter look touched his eyes. "Because of something that should never have happened. I guess that's about it. A

fool seventeen-year-old showing off before his peers said
something cruel and unwarranted. I'd like to make amends,
or try to."

I stood looking at him, a maelstrom of churning emotions. He didn't have to come, yet he had. Was I glad, or
sorry? Even as I struggled to get a grip on myself I was
aware of my attraction to him. "I've thought of it too," I
said at last. "What was said, and how. And why. But it was
all true, you know, and still is. Rivet-Eyes." I took a deep
breath. "You are the only one in this household who knows
about my—trouble. It would please me if you didn't say
anything to anyone. In this house, to others, I'm normal."

"No," he said, "no." He shook his head. "You don't
have to be afraid of anything like that, or of me. Not
anymore. If you can bring yourself to do so, perhaps what
happened in the past can be buried and we can go on from
here. I'd like to stay a while and talk."

Albert. Albert St. Denis! I managed some self-control and
when I spoke my voice was calm. "You haven't changed,"
I said, "not much, really. You're taller. You've grown up.
We were children then. We thought the whole world would
be ours. For some, I guess it turned out that way. I've done
nothing important with my life so far. What have you done
with yours, these past years?"

We moved out of the room with one accord and downstairs to the lounge. "You're different," he said. "More
assured. But also more distant. It would be harder to get to
know you."

"It might not be worthwhile if one were to try," I forced
myself to say lightly. "I have companions." At least with
him I could be myself, there were no secrets and nothing to
hide. I could feel the relief of complete honesty.

For the first time he smiled, relieving the rather sober
planes of his face. "I'd chance it," he replied gravely, and
added, "I'm looking at a beautiful woman—the most
striking woman I've ever seen with her almond eyes and
ebony hair—not a scared, hollow-eyed girl. You're the one
who's grown up."

He told me he was in the American Diplomatic Service

and had just returned from Europe. He was between assignments, but after visiting his parents in Virginia, he would be going to the Far East. I recalled he'd had two brothers, both of whom died when quite young, which left him an only child. He couldn't stay long now; he was departing at twelve o'clock for Washington, D.C.

As we settled down in armchairs the talk turned to school—individuals both of us had known, teachers, activities, though I had taken little part in those, graduation.

"I wanted to look you up right away, but lost my nerve. I kept thinking about what I'd said and how you must be feeling. One of the boys saw you as you left and I knew you'd heard. Before I could get up my courage the family moved. Then there was more schooling, all of it hard work." He paused. "Remember Stretch?"

I nodded. Half the girls in school were after Stretch Ware.

"And Tin Grin, with a mouthful of silver fillings? We weren't very kind," Albert St. Denis admitted. Then, changing the subject, he said, "I'd like to come back. Will you be here?"

"I'll be here only a week, though Madame Crecy has asked me to stay permanently, and work for her as secretary-helper."

"Why don't you? Someone else could fill your place at the library, that could be easily arranged. This would give you a secure residence and I can't think of finer surroundings. You belong here."

"Here there are those—"

"I know. But you can deal with them. Haven't you run from phantoms long enough? It has to end somewhere. This could be the answer."

I said slowly, "I can't believe how I got here. You wouldn't believe it either, if I told you. There are so many things—"

"I know," he repeated. "The way you feel, you're living two lives." He added in even tones, "You've had a hell of a time and I haven't helped. I'm more sorry than I can say about that. If people could have been a little kinder and more understanding it would have made your life easier.

This decision must rest with you, of course. But do you think you'll stay?"

"I'm not sure." I'd caught a glimpse of the clock on the wall and got to my feet reluctantly. He rose beside me. "If I do accept Madame's proposition, your encouragement will have had something to do with it."

I extended my hands and he took them in both his own. For a moment our eyes held, his were suddenly wide open, startled. Nor was I prepared for the surge of emotion that shook me at his touch, emotion that burst out of control like fire before a whirlwind.

"One meeting—after so many years—" He released me and stepped back. "Now that we've seen each other," he said quite formally, "can we meet again? I would have time to come here between my trip to Virginia and my departure for the Far East."

I nodded, wordless, and watched him leave—the lithe, clean stride, the almost military way he carried himself—and knew how much I wanted to see him again.

About to turn away I witnessed a small tableau; Jason entering as Albert left, the two passing in the broad doorway. Jason glanced at me then stared after Albert. A hard, suspicious look crossed Jason's features. Feeling no need to explain, hugging what had just happened jealously to me—and strongly unwilling to be overtaken—I walked on quickly toward the library.

CHAPTER 5

I concentrated on the books. There was a vast array of them, dealing with every subject I could have imagined, from mining and metallurgy to ancient religions and biographies of inventors, poets, and musicians. The library was a large room with a high ceiling and three of the four walls were lined with shelves.

My eye was caught by a particular volume, Hornby's *Treatise on the Occult,* and I lifted it down curiously. Skimming through the pages I noted the dearth of specific information; rather, the author seemed most impressed by himself and by whatever prestige might result from his pursuit of so weighty a subject. He'd floundered through six hundred pages to say nothing.

I turned at the sound of a voice behind me. It was Jason. "Enjoying the library? There is a pretty wide range of material here. What is that you're reading?" He peered over my shoulder. "The occult—my word, you are into it, aren't you? Do you care about that sort of thing?"

"No," I said, "I really don't," then sighed. "The book just happened to be handy and I chanced a look at it, that's all. I noticed a copy of Dolan's *The New India,* too," I added, "and a rather attractive one on archaeology. A fascinating array—one could spend hours here."

"Nothing on law?" Jason suggested.

"I didn't see anything, but I didn't get very far."

"Where there is the occult there should be ghosts," he pointed out, glancing around. "Aren't they supposed to accompany each other? I'll admit I don't know a great deal about those matters. I am suprised, though, that there is such a book here. I didn't know *Maman* was interested in the supernatural."

"I doubt she is," I replied, "she seems too practical for that. She was laughing at the possibility of the disembodied inhabiting the Old Wing, and said that if they were there they would be most unhappy at all the goings-on."

"There aren't any goings-on," Jason stated. "There has been another hangup in the renovation work, and her teeth are on edge because of it."

"I'm sorry to hear that," I said and was vaguely puzzled. "Did you finish your work sooner than expected? I thought Madame said you would be occupied all day."

"I am, actually," he admitted. "Forgot some papers, and I have to go right back. I noticed you had a guest—the gentleman I passed in the doorway, a rather tall, slim fellow. A friend, perhaps?"

I was a bit surprised that he would remark about the incident, and answered casually, "You were saying? Oh, yes. A friend. It was a very nice visit."

Had he wanted to ask further questions? I wondered after he left. To learn the identity of my caller? It shouldn't matter to him, yet his interest seemed more than idle curiosity.

The thought of Albert swept over me strongly, and I felt again the thrill I remembered. His encouragement had been heartwarming; he believed in me and was certain I could carry on. He was aware of my difficulty, had taken that into consideration, and was still certain I could cope with whatever I might have to face. His confidence in me gave me courage; and then I knew, all at once and in an instant, what my course was to be. I would give Madame Crecy an affirmative reply, and remain at the Château. There was not the slightest doubt in my mind that this was the right and proper thing to do. When Albert came again, as he said he would, he would find me here.

The next morning I presented myself at Madame's office to tell her my decision. "I did so hope that would be your answer," Madame said warmly "I am delighted!" And I could see she really was.

Any qualms I might have I'd keep to myself. Still, I would have liked to know how Yvonne came to be here; at this point all I did know was that my name was somehow a link to her. My own arrival, how it came about, was something I would not soon forget. The reason for the vision, if there was one, escaped me. So few things in my lifetime had happened without purpose!

The Mistress of Crecy must have already been up for some time, for her desk was covered with papers. The door to her inner quarters was open and I glimpsed a sitting room with Turkish rugs and deep comfortable furniture and, in a corner, a fireplace. It was cozy and inviting, with shaded lamps and books. Firelight gleamed on the polished surface of an open grand piano.

"Would you care for tea?" the old lady asked, gesturing to a pot on the table at her side. There were two cups—had she expected me? "Unless it is too soon after breakfast." She smiled. "Or I can ring for coffee, if you prefer."

"Tea will be fine," I murmured, and found it hard to believe this most pleasant personage was the same as the forbidding one of our first meeting. I accepted my cup and added by way of conversation, "This is a lovely apartment."

"I like it." The old lady was pleased. "It was my parents' when they were here, though I have had it redecorated several times and each time to my own tastes. They lived with me for a year after I was widowed. The bedroom—out of sight from where you sit—might seem heavy to most but it suits me. I have always been a large person and spindle-legged furnishings are not appropriate for me. My taste is very much the opposite of the early Victorian years, when the fashion of the day ran to fragile porcelain and rose damask, with knots of ribbon and pale pink rosebuds.

"You were an only child?"

"I am the last of my line, and so far as I know, my husband's line as well. With me, it all runs out." The depth of emotion briefly agitated her surface calm, and I realized that this matter of heritage, as Jason said, was what occupied most of her thoughts.

"I believe you told me you have no family."

"No," I said, "none."

The old lady appeared to digest this. "I see. You told me your grandfather was in trade in the Lowelton area; might I know his given name? I often do business with concerns in the United States and could have heard of him."

I hesitated, but the inquiry seemed innocent enough, and I replied. "His name was Clarence Archer. He often said he would much rather be called Archer, but it seems Clarence was a family name, and since it had been bestowed on him in his cradle, there was little he could do but bear it."

"You are from that part of the country, then."

"Not originally, no. From farther west but still within the Great Lakes vicinity. Mother was born in the South, Georgia, to be exact, but my parents met and were married in Tennessee. Father was there looking for a distant relative whose descendants were said to have settled in the area before the American Revolutionary War. He didn't find him, nor any of the others he hoped to locate—that branch of the family at least, if there was a branch, had died out. Father was greatly disappointed that he failed. It would have meant so much to him."

"And you?" inquired the Mistress of Crecy in a distant voice.

I smiled, then shook my head. "I suppose I would feel the same, if I had any relatives to worry about." And just as well I don't, I added to myself, it's better that way.

"Unfortunate. Well. Which brings me to—"

There was a peremptory knock on the door and Hilda Divino entered. "Whenever you're ready," she said then frowned as she saw me. "I didn't know you had company." Her quick eyes took in the pleasant scene with the teacups, Madame's chair drawn up close to the desk.

"I'm busy at the moment, as you can see." Madame was clearly not pleased at the interruption. "I'll let you know, but since you are here you might as well take out the dishes. And send Jeanne to me. I want to get started on the Blue Room. Have the list ready. I want a man called—I won't have the crew coming to find that door stuck."

Divino's black brows shot up. "The door's not stuck."

"You went over there?"

"I sent Francine," the woman muttered defensively. When she left it was without the dishes. Another girl retrieved them—I took her to be Jeanne—while the old lady was still shaking her head. "That Old Wing—the amount of trouble we've had getting anything done makes one wonder. Incidentally, do you notice an odd smell in here—like burned leather, or sulphur?"

For a second I couldn't answer. "N-no, but I'll open a window anyway, if you like."

The old lady had not traced it to its source, thank heaven! Before leaving, with her hand on the doorknob and her back to Madame, Hilda Divino had shot me a single piercing glance, the controlled expression on the pale countenance reflecting purest malice. She had looked at me, into my face, and something she saw there, or thought she saw, or feared, had roused her and brought up her hostility. In that moment an odor seemed to shimmer about her, as real as any aura. It was a stench that lingered.

I lifted the catch and pushed open the window, taking my time with the chore and struggling to regain my composure. Then I crossed the room again and resumed my seat.

"You were saying—?" I inquired. "Something you wanted me to do?"

"Actually, yes. As I told you, we house a rather extensive doll collection here, and it was reported to me that the case has been opened. Since I keep the case locked it is a matter of mystery to me how it could be otherwise. Probably only a mistake, someone may have only thought it was open. Nevertheless, I would like you to look in on it and see that everything is in order. The door to the Trophy Room is usually kept locked too—however, it is open right now and you won't need a key. You can report back to me, if you will. Wander about, enjoy yourself. Also would you mind dropping off these? They won't go out until morning but that's all right."

She went on to explain that mail was delivered to Crecy twice a week, which was something of a luxury since the Château was a fair distance from the city. The mail, by courtesy, was picked up from the small table downstairs just inside the front foyer.

"Of course," I said, took the letters handed me, and rose.

"You'll find the Trophy Room at the head of the long stairs on the east side."

I was at the door when her voice halted me. "Miss Kirkwood—Paulette—since you will be living here, there is something you should know. It will only take a moment." The old lady began abruptly. "It's Hilda Divino. She always has been a little strange; one of these days her temper will get the better of her. She's had a hard time. Her husband made her life miserable. He finally drank himself into a stupor and never came out of it. The fact that he didn't come out of it was a godsend long delayed, to my way of thinking. She had no money and nowhere to go so I invited her here. She's been with me ever since. That was almost twenty years ago. I call her a manager, but actually she's more than that. She keeps the wheels turning smoothly. Hilda is a strange person, quick to take offense and never forgets a slight, real or fancied. Even so, I would hate to lose her."

"She's not a relative by marriage, is she? I understood you to say you had no family at all."

"Oh no. It's a long story but I'll try to make it short. Her husband was the nephew of a gardener of mine. When he retired from my employ I learned that this person—this drunken sot—had been bleeding the old gentleman for every cent he could get, and using Hilda Divino, his wife, the same way. After he died she was at loose ends. And it has worked out, for all that her temper is something to be reckoned with at times. Since you are staying here, I feel that you should know the facts."

"I see," I said, but I didn't, not really. None of this explained the animosity the woman obviously felt toward me. But Madame had been honest, and that I did understand and appreciate. I answered her smile with one of my own, which I hoped was reassuring. "I'll see to the doll collection now," I said and went out.

I dropped the letters then made my way to the Trophy Room, a vast hall like others I'd seen in this great house.

Ranged along the paneled walls were coats of mail and armor. There were cutlasses and swords, shields and battle-axes, and knives, which I knew by their carved and inlaid handles, were extremely valuable. Standing alone in the center of the floor, holding the place of honor, was a large case constructed entirely of heavy glass and wood and aglow like a jewel from the large shaded bulb suspended directly above it. I caught the glisten of gold and the flash of gems as I stepped nearer.

There were at least fifty or more dolls of many lands, each about a foot tall and dressed in authentic costumes: Japan, all the Eastern countries; Ireland—a wee Irish lass in lace-trimmed apron—Scotland, France, even Spain and Holland. There was a plump Dutch girl and her companion, a sturdy gentleman in wooden shoes and white hose, with a flat black cap upon his flaxen head. There were kings and queens, dukes and earls in heavy robes; a monarch, bandy-legged and pompous to the point of absurdity; another, as round as a sausage with belly straining his richly furred surcoat, a tiny orb and scepter clutched in one hand, a wine glass raised high in the other. Still another, a bejeweled fop complete with gold snuffbox, wore a crown upon his curled wig. One doll I noted was a girl, Polynesian or Chinese I thought, probably both, though I couldn't tell because the features were so badly blurred. The head with the flowing black hair was flower-wreathed like something from a Gauguin painting. A long rope of the same fire-red blossoms lay between the naked breasts. She was clearly intended to be nude, but some scandalized soul had draped the voluptuous figure with a shapeless skirt down to its ankles. She had a companion, but this one was fully clothed and gorgeous in red and gold brocade: Black hair cascaded to the waist and the doll wore a coronet of sparkling jewels upon its head. The features of the latter were also blurred, evidently the work of some early artisan who had tried to improve upon the beautiful objects.

But dominating the entire collection, and most particularly the two doll-women over whom he towered, was an arrogant figure, a jeweled cutlass clutched in his huge fist and wearing pirate's boots well cuffed down. The head was thrown back in defiance and I could almost hear the

contemptuous laughter. Who, I wondered, was this imposing character who owned the world? I pulled my gaze away
almost reluctantly.

All was in order, the case securely locked as it should be, its
miniature inmates frozen in time. I turned and went back
downstairs.

Upon approaching Madame's door I halted and raised my
hand to knock, unaware at first that I was interrupting
something. The door was ajar and I couldn't help overhearing.

"Nothing is changed."

"I'll be taking orders from that girl—"

"You'll be taking orders from me. Is that understood?"

"But you're making a pet of her! Think I can't see it?
She's—"

"Here upon my invitation! And don't forget it. If I ask for
advice I'll expect advice, otherwise go on as you have. Is
that understood?"

"I don't like it. It means nothing but trouble with her
around. I won't be interfered with! I don't—"

They were talking about me! My face burned. I didn't know
what to do; certainly I couldn't enter Madame's office now.
I'd eavesdropped, not intentionally, but that didn't change
matters.

Suddenly the door burst wide and Divino charged out. I
moved aside or she would have bowled me over. I watched
her stride angrily down the hall, a drift of scorch wafting
back to me, and did I see, faintly, an aura?

There was something very wrong here, very bad; more
than temper or ill will, but something dangerous and to be
feared. Was this the Evil Yvonne meant? Coldness grew in
my inner being, threatening to engulf me.

For a long moment I stood, forcing myself to calmness and
rationality. Was what I'd heard the key to Divino's resentment?

She had accused me of coming here to take over. How
could she think such a thing? Divino had served Madame
these many years; certainly Divino had nothing to fear from
outsiders. Then why would it make any difference who
Madame Crecy hired, or who came to the Château? I wasn't

here to displace anyone. How could I? The idea was preposterous.

I meant to keep my distance as much as I could, it was not my intention to cause any disruptions in this household. But the old lady's words came back to haunt me, pressing insistently upon my consciousness, ringing in my ears like the tolling of a bell: *Hilda never forgets a slight, real or fancied—*

There was trouble ahead and I knew it.

CHAPTER 6

At the moment it would have been difficult to face Madame.
I wandered about for a while then paused in the doorway of
the Music Room. Here was where Albert and I had met, and
I would have loved to linger, but the room was occupied.
The little old lady at the piano was making hard work of
Mozart but her audience loyally cheered her on. A gray head
turned, curls bobbed, I was offered a sweet smile and a
waggle of the fingers before I withdrew.

I chose a current magazine from a rack of reading
material in the lounge and went upstairs to my quarters.
Laying the magazine aside, I washed my face and smoothed
my hair. My clothing had arrived and, since the day was
warm, I decided to change into something more in keeping
with the weather. Perhaps a crisp white shirtwaist with a
broad collar and pale green buttons at the cuffs and down
the front. I had just such a waist, all I had to do was reach
in and get it.

I opened the closet door and stepped back, surprised to
see a heap of rags on the floor. They appeared to be strips
of old blanket or toweling. There was a perfectly logical
explanation, I was sure. With so many serving girls at
Crecy, so many cleaning ladies and chambermaids, one of
them, in pursuit of her tasks, had merely dropped the rags,
meaning to pick them up later. I'd leave them as they were.

I backed out, stopped, then looked again. It struck me as

odd that the pile should be there at all. Nothing was ever out of place at Crecy. I was learning that Madame couldn't abide what she termed sloppiness, and she wouldn't like this. But my simple deduction still satisfied me, and I put the incident from my mind. However, I had no further urge to change my shirtwaist.

Returning to the lounge I tucked the unread magazine back into the rack, and went on to Madame's office.

"Did you make the tour? Find something of interest?"

"Very much. The display is dazzling."

Madame smiled. "My dear, relax, enjoy. And never worry about working for me, we'll get along. Would you mind? That box on the chair—"

"This one?" It was a heavy affair, metal and metal-bound—fireproof, I thought, a container of the sort one kept valuables in. This seemed to be full of pictures, old prints, newspaper clippings, and documents yellowed with age. The lid was open and I carefully closed it before extending the box to Madame.

She shook her head. "No, put it in the safe there on the wall. You're stronger than I am, and more agile. Just put it inside and close the door—there," she said as I complied, "that's it. The lock will take care of the rest. Now would you like to stay with me for a while to familiarize yourself with what needs to be done? Or do you have other plans?"

I didn't, and said so. The many places I wanted to explore in this old house could wait; besides, I would not have felt free to invade any of them unless given clearance to do so. I was not that familiar with Crecy yet.

"You'll want to hear about the doll collection," I told her. "Everything looked fine, each doll appeared to be in its place, and the case was securely locked, I didn't see anything that might have been disturbed."

Madame nodded in satisfaction. "I thought as much but still it is well to keep track of such things." She reached for a pen. I watched her make entries in a ledger, and was pleased that she seemed inclined to talk.

She spoke of her childhood and her youth, and of her husband's family, which I gathered at one time had been quite extensive. She was born and grew up in France, where she met and married Lionel, the young scion of Crecy. The marriage was brief; he was killed in an accident when on a visit to France. She'd taken over the estate and managed it ever since.

"For a young widow, it must not have been easy," I remarked.

"No." The old lady paused and seemed to be remembering back. "It wasn't," she said briefly. "That was an interesting first year." Her mood lightened; she laughed. "I think the biggest problem was my parents. They were hesitant to leave their home in France but were stubbornly convinced their daughter needed their guidance and supervision." She waved a hand. "So long ago, all past history. You didn't say what trade your grandfather was in."

I answered readily enough. "He worked for an importing firm in his younger years, then bought them out. I believe he managed it for some time but eventually sold it." I mentioned that my father died when I was ten, Mother soon after, that Grandfather put me through school, and when I became old enough I'd kept house for him.

I expected more questions but there were none. As before, it wasn't the discussion of immediate relatives I feared—immediate meaning my grandfather—but one thing often led to another. Not far enough back was my ill-fated great-uncle Herman, also possessed of the gift, but unable to cope with it. A knotted rope in an attic put an end to him.

"It's late," the old lady was saying, "and I haven't had lunch yet. I assume you've had yours?" When I nodded, she said, "Then maybe you can join me in a tart and coffee—coffee at least. That bellpull there by the door . . . ? Fine. I'll be with you in a minute," she added, "just make yourself at home." She began gathering papers, stacking them in neat piles, then drew an account book forward.

I moved to the window. From where I stood I could see the end of the ramp, and beyond it green grass, a fountain, potted plants, a large ornamental tree in an enormous jardiniere. Rustic seats were scattered about, one near a delightfully cool-looking thicket and a pool. There would be goldfish in the pool and, a little later in the season, pink waterlilies on those green pads. I caught a glimpse of delphiniums and daisies just beginning to bloom, while primroses and pansies provided a burst of color along the cobblestone walks.

My back was still turned when Mrs. Divino answered the summons. "My lunch is to be served here in the office," the old lady instructed. "It needn't take you long to get it, since I know what we're serving and I'll have the same. Onion soup, a salad of fruit, cheese. And tarts and coffee for two." She emphasized this; I purposely kept my head averted. The manager's stubborn silence was self-explanatory.

"For two."

"I heard!" the manager retorted and slammed the door on her way out.

"Churlish lump," the old lady muttered half under her breath and I hid a smile. I didn't turn until she spoke again. "I saw you looking at my garden. And what do you think of it?"

I took the chair indicated, near the desk. "Beautiful," I said warmly, "and I'm running out of superlatives. It suits Crecy perfectly. Truly an enchanting retreat."

Madame nodded. "One of my favorite spots. The pool is particularly nice, I think."

When the meal came, someone else brought it, and instead of the requested coffee, there was tea.

The old lady's eyes blazed. "Don't tell me this is a simple mistake! I've a good mind to send it back with a reprimand. On my soul, I don't know what gets into that woman sometimes. She heard me well enough, she just wants to be contrary."

"It doesn't matter," I murmured. I'd had the same beverage for my own lunch, but it wouldn't have made any difference anyway. Yet I wondered about Divino.

The tarts were delicious as I'd known they would be, despite the flagrant ill will displayed in serving.

"More?" Madame pushed the dainty teapot forward but I shook my head. The drink had been delicious, some robust

English blend, I judged. I set my fragile cup and saucer down carefully.

"Pretty, aren't they?" she remarked. "I've had them for years. I'm always afraid a tenant will let his teeth slip and bite a piece out of one of those cups."

I stared. "You mean these—cups like this—are in common use at the tables?"

The old lady laughed. "Yes, why not? Precious things are meant to be enjoyed, not hoarded. That's why I have thrown my home open to others."

I was beginning to like her very much. She was totally lacking in artifice, as mentally alert as a woman less than half her age, and had a sharp, unexpected, and thoroughly delightful sense of humor. I found the Mistress of Crecy fascinating.

When we had finished our lunch, she asked, "Would you like to try your hand at this? There is a drop-leaf on that side of the desk, pull it up and I'll explain what is to be done." The table holding the luncheon things was pushed back and ledgers produced.

There were also letters; three were to tradesmen, another in reply to a notice of property offered for sale at a discount—the reply was brief, businesslike, and negative. A fifth letter was to accompany a check for holly and decorations for the most recent holiday; I gathered it had been a gala festivity, with many guests. I noted the amount of the check, and sighed. It must have been stupendous.

"Jason was supposed to have mailed this from his office," Madame remarked. "I've had a reminder that he did not. An oversight of course, but I don't fancy delinquent accounts, not under any circumstances. I'm including an apology."

Late afternoon was shattered by a frenzied knocking on the door. I opened it to a serving girl whose tear-stained face worked convulsively. She had tomato juice—or what appeared to be tomato juice—splattered all down her front, and her apron was half ripped off, the jaunty cap askew.

"*Madame— s'il vous plaît*! Look at me! *Regardez-moi*! From now on I take orders no more from zat—zat—"

"Marie, what's the trouble?" Madame's voice cracked like a whip. "Stop blubbering, girl! And speak French if it bothers you that much." The girl was wringing her hands as she worked herself up to a fresh outburst. There followed a flood of French so rapid I doubted I could have kept up with it, even had I been fluent in the language.

Madame set her jaw ominously. "Go back to your post," she said after hearing the girl out. "Return to your work, do as well as you can, and mind your own business. Do you understand—*comprenez-vous*? I give the orders, not Madame Divino. I am the authority here! If there is any more difficulty, any at all, come to me at once."

"Madame—the Divino"—the girl choked, her face still flaming with outrage, "she ees not herself these days, I theenk. Why? She ees crazee, sick in ze head. *Elle est folle, je crois.*"

"Very well, that will do! Now get on about your chores." I watched her dismiss the girl firmly.

"Hilda," the old lady growled. "One of these days she'll push me too far."

How Marie had run afoul of the manager I didn't know, but there had obviously been a pitched battle, hand to hand, from the look of it. Somehow it was difficult to picture the dark, stern woman hurling a pot of tomatoes. Could it have been because Divino was so upset at my being here? No, that was unlikely. These clashes must have occurred before. Yet if it was my arrival that had sparked off the anger, and she was taking it out on the help because of me, it could mean accelerated trouble for the house, and thus for Madame herself. It was a possibility I shuddered to contemplate. Ill will directed toward me was one thing; for it to affect others, and especially this old lady, was something else.

She wrote checks for two deliveries, one for laundry and another for wallpaper, and she initialed the statements which I filed away under her supervision.

At three o'clock the girl Celeste came with coffee and cookies. "Or," Madame asked, "would you prefer to go downstairs for a break?"

"No, I'd rather stay here."

"You seem preoccupied. Is anything the matter?"

I felt myself flush. "I'm sorry if I've been slow. I probably should have been paying more attention."

"No, you're doing fine," the old lady said. "I'm well pleased. What did you think of the doll collection?" she added. "You didn't say. The collection is what everyone who knows of it wants to inspect first."

"It's lovely," I said and with an effort put my worries aside.

"Which one did you like best?" A smile tugged at the corners of the old lady's mouth.

"Well—" I paused. "The girl with the flowers in her hair."

"Ah. That was old Thomas's wife, Manona. She poisoned him, you know, bloodthirsty little witch. She died by the same means, no one knows whether it was by her own hand or not. There are two figures of her in the case—before and after. Before and after civilization, that is."

I had to laugh. "I notice somebody civilized her, all the way down to her ankles. I've never seen anything so hideous in my life as that shapeless bag—on her, I mean."

Madame's chuckle joined mine. "I agree. The second likeness is quite a work of art, or was, before someone who thought he could do better tried and failed. Both are mutilated, and two others besides, a Spanish nobleman and a Manchurian prince. The Manchurian is so fat the mutilation can pass unnoticed."

I finished my coffee, brushed away the crumbs, and sat waiting for Madame's further instructions.

"That Holbein is not back yet," she stated abruptly. "They take forever to complete their work. Pangborn's the best in the business but he takes his time. He can afford to. And I couldn't afford not to use him. That Holbein is well over three hundred years old and even good portraits become fragile eventually. The shop will be closed now but you can write him a note first thing in the morning. I mean to ask him how much longer he intends to take."

She was slipping into the role of employer with me, and I was happy to have it so. "I'll do that," I agreed.

A messenger came to the door, entered, and spoke to her briefly.

I paid little attention to the conversation, but presently Madame nodded, her voice flat. "All right—all right. Tell him I'll want to see it anyway, of course. The same old thing," she muttered as the door closed and we were alone again. "Well, that's all for now. Jason will be along shortly and I have something I want to discuss with him."

I went out, having in mind a visit to the largest of Crecy's galleries. I passed no one in the halls and, so far as I knew, no one passed me. The house was quiet. Where was Yvonne, over on the other side where she preferred to be?

The small gallery down on the first floor was being renovated and would not be finished; the one I was heading toward, bore evidence of recent overhauling. The huge double doors were open, with the protective canvas still spread on the floor. There was the odor of fresh varnish and paint and clean polished wood.

With no artistic ability to speak of, I nevertheless appreciated fine paintings and knew that the mansion boasted some masterpieces; old masters, Jason had told me. Among those represented downstairs in the smaller main floor gallery I would later visit were Botticelli and Van Dyck. There were also contemporary works, her prize, one by Degas, recently arrived from Paris. Madame, he said, had done her share of collecting in past years, and in addition to the numerous portraits of her ancestors and those of her husband, she had favored the Spanish painter Velasquez, and owned several of his works.

Space in plenty was needed for such displays, and this room was huge, its walls hung with paintings in every conceivable type of frame. And the works were in excellent condition; paint glowed with uncanny depth and vibrancy. The subjects almost appeared to breathe. One large portrait was missing. Idly I wondered whose it was.

A particular painting drew me. It was a portrait of the same man whose likeness I'd seen on one of the dolls, but here his image was life-sized. This had to be the famed Thomas of Crecy, the founder of the house.

Swarthy and broad, with the shine of Lucifer in his eyes, he was most richly and flamboyantly dressed in the fashion of day. On his little finger, left hand, he wore a ring of curious make—multiple interwoven strands of gold set with a magnificent ruby supported on either side by large opals. Only a true artist would have combined the two. Even I knew of the fragility of the opal, while a ruby was akin to a diamond and almost its equal in hardness. Yet here the ruby and the far gentler opal had been combined deliberately, defiantly.

Nearby was a fragile, almost ethereal beauty with meditative eyes, a woman gowned in sea green satin, her face, framed by pale gold hair, delicate in the extreme, her expression sweetly withdrawn. Clearly she didn't belong beside the swashbuckler, the strong man who defied convention.

There were others and I studied them briefly. In a larger dark wood frame I saw two youngsters at a matronly knee, one bearing the inevitable stamp of his swarthy ancestor; this boy, the mother held grimly. The second child, slim and serious, showed a distinct resemblance to the sea green lady. If this represented the other side of the clan, certainly the two must have mixed uneasily, like oil and water. The dark strain was strongest, showing up in the ink black hair or heavy brows, the knowing eyes or the sardonic, ready-for-anything expression which shouted aloud that the bearer would do as he pleased and the devil be damned. The smooth-paneled wall was empty without the missing likeness and again I wondered whose it could be.

I stood a moment longer, drawn by the magnetism of Old Thomas. He might almost be alive, I marveled, the likeness was so realistic. In the next moment he'd open his mouth with a bull's roar, stride from his great gilt frame to trample everything in his path. A magnificent specimen, this builder of empires, with full sensuous lips and eyes glinting with rollicking devilry. Even as I watched, did a heavy eyelid droop in a wink? Though I felt fleeting sympathy for the

distance we had already come, inquired, "Aren't we going to get there pretty soon?"

"It's not far now, and I must say that I am enjoying the company. Actually, I've no idea how things look from here on, so it will be something new for both of us."

Again I made no reply. We had reached the hallway's end, turned a corner and were brought up against what appeared to be a blank wall.

"This way. Through this door." I ducked under a strip of tarpaulin and passed through the heavy doors held open for me. "Be careful of your footing. Confound it, it's dark in this place! Why didn't they leave that west window uncovered, at least?"

But I had paused, listening. There was something wrong here, something awry. I had become immediately conscious of activity, of voices. Unhappy voices, sad voices, and one had risen above the others, weeping. Through a far doorway, the wall surrounding it half stripped of its facings, I could see the vague outline of furniture. Then as my vision cleared, I saw that everything in that section was in excellent condition and in good order. A table twenty or more feet in length occupied the center of the long room, with polished high-back chairs arranged precisely around it. So there was where they would be gathered. Here where I stood beside Jason was only dust and decay; swaying cobwebs hung from strips of ceiling and dangled from the rafters.

"Well, you can't see much," Jason said disappointedly. His voice reverberated in the gloom. "I led you on a real wild-goose chase. Want to go back?"

"In a minute."

"What's the matter?"

I shook my head. Something still troubled me. From the greater darkness to our right came a measured tap-tap-tap.

"That?"

"No. It's probably the wind, loose canvas or a board outside. Is there another way to get in?"

"To this part? Yes. To the right of the house from the front walk. A below-ground-level entry. It was the old opening to the dungeon, built in the seventeen hundreds. They had malefactors in those days, too. Some fled with the onset of the French Revolution. A few became law-abiding citizens, others were caught by the retribution they had avoided back home. Crecy took care of its own.''

"I—see," I said.

"Afraid?"

"No. Why on earth should I be afraid? There's nothing to be afraid of." I stood for a little while longer looking, feeling. Again it struck me as odd, the difference between this part and that beyond, the latter existing in an almost perfect state of preservation. No dry rot there, no dust. No cobwebs. One would have had to reach it by climbing on scaffolding, unless there was still another entrance. I asked and received an affirmative reply. Yes, but it was a long way around. Nor was this by any means all of the Old Wing. One floor yonder was made up of ballrooms, dining halls, and audience chambers, all in generally good condition— nothing like this. There was an el extension containing solars, garderobes, and sleeping areas, most of the latter small, cramped cubbyholes.

"But they went all out for their pleasures," Jason added. "They did not skimp on the ballrooms."

"Is that the banquet hall, where that enormous table is? I can see armor and banners on the walls. Strange they wouldn't have been covered, against the dust."

Jason was silent. "They were," he said then. "Some-body's carelessness, of course. Should be mentioned to *Maman,* though she's quite upset already with the delays."

Delays, I thought, and then I had it. Delays. No wonder, I thought. The unhappiness, the air of the place. The others Yvonne spoke of were clinging to what they knew and didn't want to give it up. There was resistance, all right, a feeling stronger and more distinct here than in any other part of the house. Here entities moved freely. There would be the rustle of silk and the thin crackle of parchment, the clink of sword and heavy tread of men's boots. I had an uneasy sensation that we shouldn't be here.

"Don't look down," Jason said, "you'll get dizzy." His

arm touching my shoulders, steadying me, became a gentle pressure; I turned to move back and suddenly found myself teetering over empty space.

"Watch out!" It was a warning that almost came too late; he reached for me and missed. I flung my arms out wildly for something to cling to and avoid being sucked down into those dark depths. My flailing hands struck an upright and I clutched frantically even as he pulled me to safety.

"My God! You almost tumbled through that hole! I was afraid of this. I should never have brought you here in the first place. It's too dangerous! Are you all right?"

I looked behind me. Inches away was that yawning hole; three missing boards and a sickening drop had opened up to the floor far below, with its dim litter of scaffolding, ladders, and scattered lumber. I swallowed hard, clinging to my post. "I'm—fine," I managed. "I want to go back now, though."

"I shouldn't wonder! Great God—I blame myself entirely. It was my fault that—"

"No—really," I said in a steadier tone, now that my legs were not trembling as much. "I'm all right. I shouldn't have stepped back when I did—I must have caught my heel on something. Thanks for rescuing me."

"Almost didn't," he growled. "One split second more and it would have been all over. With that much of a drop, you'd have been killed. If anything had happened to—"

"Nothing did, so stop worrying," I said as we retraced our steps. "It is a grand old place, especially this part, and well worth seeing. Really full of memories," I added, but I was definitely more comfortable when we reached solid footing.

Jason appeared thoughtful and subdued, and once back in the lighted hallway he drew a breath of relief. He stopped at a narrow oriel window, looking down. "I want you to see this; the view is calm and pleasant and might help to settle your nerves. This old mausoleum is full of views, as you know, but this is one you might have missed."

Below, an ancient cobbled walk and part of a west tower were visible, the walk overgrown with weeds and the straggled canes of some unkempt plant; at the base of a gnarled tree were the remnants of a semicircular garden seat of weathered stone.

"I wonder how many trysts have been kept there?"

I would have walked on but he was still blocking my way. "It is old," I murmured. "Perhaps quite a few."

"Paulette," he said and suddenly came close to lay a hand on my arm. "I haven't known you very long but you have become very important to me. As a matter of fact I think I'm already half in—When I thought I'd lost you back there—"

"I'm sorry. I believe I would like to sit down. Reaction, no doubt," I said, prompted not by the tremors in my legs but by the sudden wave of weakness that swept over me at his words. I pushed past him and on to the dining room.

He was instantly contrite. "Of course! How thoughtless of me! You've had a narrow escape and will take a while to recover. They are beginning to serve, let me find us a table. Perhaps some good hot food—you see I feel I should look after you, particularly after having put you in a position that nearly ended your life."

I bit my lips, feeling the weakness recede. "It was just an accident and best forgotten."

"Then you don't hold it against me?"

"No, naturally not, how could I, when it was my own fault?"

He pulled out a chair and I sat down; he seated himself opposite me. Inwardly I sighed. This man was warm and supportive and likable, yet a memory intruded; a memory of someone tall, with a fine, sensitive face, someone I had known long ago and was coming to know again. I jerked myself free of my wayward thoughts.

"Do you feel all right now?" Jason was saying.

"Yes, thank you."

"And what did you do with your day, that is, before we went back to the Old Wing?" He was being polite, obviously trying to make conversation.

"I kept busy," I said. "I visited the gallery, the large one, and found it fascinating. I wandered around."

"According to *Maman,* you'll be staying at Crecy."

I looked up from my consommé. "She told you?"

"I asked her. I rather expected you would, you know. She can be persuasive. And she's taken very much of a fancy to you, which clearly doesn't please the Gorgon much."

"The what?"

"Divino. She's jealous."

"Jealous? Oh, I don't think so," I said quickly.

"Why not? It is true." Jason shook his head. "Actually, she has no business being at Crecy at all, she's worn out her welcome. Because twenty years ago *Maman* extended charity, does she still have to put up with her?"

The bitter denunciation startled me. The conversation was getting out of hand and, frankly, I didn't know what to say. I'd known he didn't like Mrs. Divino but had no idea he felt this strongly.

"I'm sure she wouldn't keep her on if she didn't want to," I said mildly. "Shouldn't one try to see it from Madame Crecy's viewpoint? What is best for her is what counts."

"It's what's best for her that I am thinking of."

"But she sets great store by her manager, and if it is her choice—"

"Self-styled manager," Jason insisted. "Anyone can do what Divino does. You don't know the woman. She's a troublemaker. And *Maman*'s will is written in her favor."

I was even more puzzled. "But I don't understand. If—"

"Divino need not be here to inherit," Jason stated bluntly. "The household would be better off without her. I urged *Maman* to discharge her long ago, but she wouldn't; I told her again just yesterday. That mistaken sense of obligation! Well, obligation doesn't extend that far."

It was useless to point out to Jason that he was wrong, that it was Madame herself who determined her own needs and those of the household. Moreover, even though he handled a share of her affairs, I didn't think he had the right to impress his views upon her. She'd given no intimation she needed that kind of advice, which to her must be an annoyance, possibly even a concern. Should she be burdened with such a concern?

I was relieved when he changed the subject. "That old section—it looks pretty bad, doesn't it? And *Maman* can't get anything done. For the amount of money she's spent on it already, something should have been accomplished. If it were mine I'd leave it as it is and concentrate on this part. Here is where the tenants are, and here is where the business is."

You and the ghosts would prefer it that way, I could have said, but settled for replying, "I don't know. I truly don't. Actually, I have no opinion on the matter at all; the only thing I do believe is that the decisions about the Château should be left up to the person who owns it."

"Yes," Jason agreed briefly, "I suppose so." I could feel him studying me, my face, my hair. "I have never known anyone like you." He spoke in a rapid, excited way. "I cannot help admiring your eyes—velvet black with a hint of purple in a certain light." He made as if to reach across the table but I drew back. Once more I felt a surge of annoyance.

"I thought we agreed not to discuss my eyes anymore."

He was quick to reply. "I can only say what I think. If I am too bold, too forward, do forgive me."

He had said the same thing before. Maybe I could put an end to the subject, once and for all. "You just don't understand," I said slowly. "I've heard this sort of comment all my life and it really bothers me. It is very possible I am a throwback, the slanted eyes a legacy from a seafaring ancestor who plied the China trade. But I am not so very different from anyone else, and would like to be treated so."

"I see," he said, but if he was surprised at my disclosure he failed to show it. "It's just that I admire you tremendously, although you do keep a man at arms' length. Nevertheless I regret my idle words. A truce?" The apology was not genuine; he was not chagrined at all, I saw, only smilingly certain I would accept his offer. I shrugged and put the matter aside, reminding myself again that here was someone who wanted everything his way; it was his nature to persist despite being rebuffed.

We chatted for a few moments longer, then I bid him

good night, almost tiptoeing when I went upstairs. Evenings for Madame's people meant gathering in the music room, or the library, or the lounge, reminiscing or dreaming until the hour for bed. Lights out, for them, came early.

The first thing I did upon reaching my room was to look in the closet; the rags were gone as I had expected they would be. The only mystery in this house, I chided myself, was of my own making.

I'd had a brief note from Andrea, the missive penned shortly before she sailed. It was addressed to the hotel, and it had traveled a roundabout route, to be at last forwarded here. In it she expressed sadness that we might not see each other again since it seemed best, upon reaching England, to remain there because of her mother's delicate health. But please write, she requested me, and very soon.

I had written once and now thought I'd write again. It might cheer her. Also she should know where I was and that I intended to stay. I gave a sigh for the memory of our past good times, and turned to the small desk where ink and pens and paper were kept. It was then that I noticed the glass of water. It was my habit from childhood to leave a tumbler of water on the bedside table in case I wanted it during the night.

I reached for the glass to lift it to my lips and, without realizing how I did so, knocked it over. The liquid dripped from the table, saturating the carpet. Aghast at my clumsiness, I hastily mopped the table then looked about for something, anything, in which to put the splintered pieces of glass. Then I paused, frowning. I had emptied that tumbler this morning, rinsed it and placed it in the bathroom beside the washbasin, hadn't I? Or, my mind on other things, had I only *thought* I'd taken the glass away? I tried to remember; was it there when I came to the room to change my shirtwaist? I wasn't sure.

I got to my feet, staring at the wet spot on the rug, then rang for a maid. When the girl came I asked her if she had put the glass on the table. She looked bewildered.

"But *mademoiselle*," she protested, "I deed not breeng ze water—*non*! I do nothing up here—I deliver nothing. I work in laundry room—*j'ai passé toute la journée à la blanchisserie! Mais non, ce n'était moi!''* She had been working in the laundry room all day. It could not have been she!

The girl paused, shrugged, looked excitedly about, shrugged again in her effort to make Mademoiselle understand. *She* had not brought the glass! She had brought nothing, delivered nothing. It must be someone else. Was it water or some kind of juice in the tumbler? She darted over and examined the wet spot, then before I could stop her touched a finger to it and then to her tongue. She made a wry face.

"Pthah! *C'est ne pas de l'eau,''* she chattered excitedly, "eet ees not water—you onnerstand? Celeste breeng nothing, you ask maybe ze other maids eef zey breeng—not Celeste. Ees strong stoff. Tastes fonny,'' she concluded, big-eyed, and backed hurriedly to the door.

"Wait,'' I said. Wouldn't it be better to smooth over the situation until I could figure it out for myself? There was no use frightening the girl. I smiled, then shrugged and pointed to the nightstand. "I'm sure I left it there and forgot about it.'' I explained that I often took water to bed with me, and sometimes when I felt a little cold coming on, I added cough medicine to it. "Whoever cleaned the room thought I wanted it left there,'' I said, "then just now I knocked it over. Yes, that was what happened.''

"Oui!'' The girl's eyes cleared in relief. She curtsied, sunnily smiling. "*Oui. Je comprends.* Ees that. *Alors.* I go now, will send someone to clean up, eh? *Très bien.''* She bobbed another curtsy, then vanished. I closed the door slowly after her. I was in the bathtub when a second servant arrived to clear away the litter.

When I returned to the room all evidence of the mishap was gone, and I was no nearer an explanation than before.

But doubts grew; the more I thought about it the more certain I was that I *had* removed that glass. Slowly I realized that only by accidentally knocking over the glass, had I avoided the harm intended to me. For why should anyone go to the trouble of placing something within my reach, a tumbler containing something other than it should have, unless it was to have some sinister effect?

Not Divino. Divino wouldn't do this, wouldn't dare. Yet I couldn't shake myself free of the vivid recollection of resentment so strong it actually had an odor, of the black looks, the snatch of conversation I'd overheard outside Madame's door.

Divino would have keys to all these suites, but she didn't service the rooms. Maids did that. Nothing else in the suite appeared to be disturbed, yet upon looking in the top drawer of the dresser for a handkerchief, I found the drawer's contents disarranged. A box of sachet was not where I'd left it; a small box of hairpins and a sewing kit had tumbled beneath hosiery.

So it could have been a maid after all. But I didn't know for sure. I only knew I wouldn't run to Madame with the problem; with the increasing unrest in the kitchens, she was having trouble enough of her own. I would dispense with keeping water on the bedside table; I seldom used it anyway.

I dreamed that night. A nightmare in which I walked too near the brink of an abyss, the dark depths sucking at my feet, with terror fighting to burst from my throat. And behind me there was someone, faceless, voiceless, but a presence nonetheless, a pressure urging me gently, so gently but insistently, closer to the brink—

I struggled awake, my body bathed in perspiration and so hopelessly entangled in the bedclothes it was difficult to extricate myself.

What a horrible dream! It had no meaning, no significance—how could it have? I was just wrought up from when I'd nearly fallen this afternoon. But for a long time I sat stiffly upright in bed staring into space, the lamp on the bedside table blazing brightly.

CHAPTER 8

~∞~

To my relief, I'd been able to avoid seeing Divino. It was possible I'd jumped to conclusions about her; the idea that she had been in my suite, concocting some sort of a death potion, was foolishness. To a degree at least, I'd allowed my own personal dislike of the woman to cloud my judgment. This I tried to tell myself, and for my own peace of mind and for the sake of my work, put my suspicions aside.

Daily I was becoming more familiar with what I was expected to do, and more at ease with it. Some of the bookkeeping Madame hired out, but I couldn't help marveling that the old lady kept her finger so securely on the affairs of the household. She did all the ordering and wrote, personally, all the checks for incoming goods; she settled disputes, gave advice, even extended credit when necessary and ruled over her domain like the autocrat she was. I had the utmost admiration for her.

Trucks, carts, and wagons came and went at the delivery entrances, and working with the invoices I gained some conception of the vast amount of supplies involved—linens, utilities, foodstuffs. The bill for fresh milk alone was astronomical, not to mention buttermilk, cheeses, and the like.

Madame also kept in close contact with her employees. She not only knew the exact number of servants employed but called everyone by his or her first name and knew to the penny what each was paid. She also knew the preferences of her guests, most of whom had been with her for years and probably would be for the rest of their lives.

Jason dropped in frequently, sometimes for only a few minutes, other times on business, bringing papers for her to inspect or to sign. And he had taken to coming quite early in the day.

Sometimes I caught the old lady looking at me strangely, not in an unkind fashion, but as if she meant to ask something then thought better of it. And when Jason was present, leaning over her shoulder, perched familiarly upon a corner of her desk or relaxing in a chair, she watched us both, though her hooded eyes revealed nothing. What was she really thinking? I wondered.

One morning, and it was a special morning for me, I chanced to be near the foyer at mail delivery time and spied what I had long awaited—a particular envelope with my name on it, postmarked Washington D.C., U.S.A. My heart leaped—it was from Albert!

As I started to turn away, Jason's voice hailed me. "Paulette, good morning! Oh, has the post arrived already? It's early." He reached for the stack of letters and sorted through it, for mail often came to Crecy for him.

"I'll take these up to *Maman*," he suggested, "I want to see her anyway." He watched me with curiosity, I thought, and with something else in his eyes that I couldn't define, but his smile was frank and disarming. "Are you coming now? We can go together."

"I'll be along in a few minutes," I said, and moved on. I found a seat in the lounge and swiftly opened my letter. It was brief, and I read eagerly.

Dear Paulette:

It was a pleasure to see you again, and to enjoy your company if only for a short while.

I hope this finds you well, and still at the Château. At any rate I shall take that chance, and trusting that the time suggested will not be inconvenient, I will visit you there sometime during the latter part of the week of May 25. I am scheduled to leave on my next assignment very shortly but wanted to see you before I go. It was signed simply, *Albert.*

This was now the first part of the week; he would perhaps come Thursday or Friday, then. I ran my fingers over the note, the excitement that I had not known for so very, very long, possessing me again. I might have been back in school all those years ago, waiting to catch a glimpse of him, wondering if he would speak to me, or even pass my way. I could have been that young girl again, alive with the same eagerness, the thrill of anticipation. He had been in my thoughts and dreams so much of late!

The glow must have remained, for the old lady remarked quite casually, "Good news?"

Warmth touched my cheeks, but I answered frankly. "Well—yes. A gentleman friend of mine is coming to call."

"The same one who called before? A fine-looking young man."

And I thought she hadn't noticed! I might have known she wouldn't miss anything—she'd viewed us from the balcony of course, her favorite observation point. But I didn't feel she was prying, and I didn't mind.

"Yes," I said, "the same one." I explained something of Albert's background and that we had gone to school together, that he was in the Diplomatic Service and would soon leave for the Far East.

She said abruptly, "What about Jason? He's leading you toward the altar."

I had no reply, and the moment passed. I wouldn't have known what to tell her; only that Jason was a good conversationalist, knowledgeable, and pleasant to be with.

"Ah, yes," she murmured, "those faraway places, exotic and unattainable. To frequent such places was one of Lionel's and my dreams, but circumstances did not work out that way." She shook her head, sighed, and became practical. "You have never been down to my garden, and it is very nice. We have had a rather severe winter but springtime is making up for it. Why don't you take your friend there when he comes? You can visit undisturbed.'' It was a very nice and thoughtful suggestion; she had realized that I might appreciate privacy.

I'd not learned what had put the old lady in the wheelchair in the first place, somehow it was not that important. I lost sight of the chair completely when I was with her; a dominant personality transcended mechanical contrivances. Occasionally I'd been asked to wheel her here or there, a chore I was always happy to perform. But we'd not yet visited her garden, and now she had offered it to me, her personal retreat. I was touched, and thanked her warmly.

Tradesmen and salespeople often called upon her, and when two gentlemen presented themselves that same afternoon I attached no significance to it. What was unusual was that Jason accompanied them. A business meeting, I judged, and absented myself accordingly.

What better opportunity to explore an area I'd especially wanted to see? This time I would go to the West Wing, at least a part of it.

"There is a particularly nice solar," Madame had told me when I'd mentioned my plans, "at the head of the west stairs, and a garderobe just off that." She'd cautioned me to be careful of protruding nails; the old privy had been closed off, and its door was boarded up. And the balcony, the one extending out over the courtyard, was not safe, so under no circumstances was I to venture out upon it. Otherwise the floor, stairways, and railings in that part of the house were sound.

There was a conservatory on this same floor I wanted to see, but decided against it. Some other time. I hadn't been this far upstairs before and felt a bit out of place—more so when I looked up and beheld the figure bearing down upon me. I would have swung aside but could not; Mrs. Divino cut me off, obviously with the intention of provoking an argument.

"What are you doing up here?"

Startled as I was, a curt reply was on the tip of my tongue; instead, I answered calmly. "I've been given permission to visit the premises, Mrs. Divino, whenever I like. I'm not bothering you.''

Her gaze slid past me. "You think you know your way around, young miss? You haven't begun. Did Madame tell you about the solar, and the big balcony? From that balcony you can see halfway across the city. Did she tell you that?'' The voice was insinuating; I turned cold with the implication of her words.

"Madame *warned* me," I managed and brushed past the woman and went on. The odor lingered, stronger than before; the hot sulphurous stench lay thick on the air, constricting my throat and making breathing difficult. I shivered. Looking back I found her gone, the hallway empty. She had a way of swooping in like a black crow about to peck one's eyes out. The comparison was a chilling one.

Mindful of the old lady's directions I took the small stairs, turned off and found myself in a large room. A door led to still another hall, dim enough so I was forced to move slowly to orient myself. Proceeding under an archway I came into a spacious and airy apartment lighted on one side by tall, multipaned windows. Here too there were no cobwebs, no dust, only the brittle smell of age, of dignity and mystery.

Again stairs were ahead of me and I climbed them slowly, savoring the feel of the smooth ancient wood banister beneath my fingers, then bypassed the boarded door of which Madame had spoken and came at last to the top and the old solar.

From the solar, a small semicircular room facing westward for greatest exposure to sunshine, a wide-open door led to the balcony. And here I was shocked to see, seated well out upon it with her back to me, a young woman calmly combing her hair. She wore a loose-fitting garment and brightly colored slippers on her feet. I could see where the robe trailed upon the warped floorboards and I started forward, alarmed. Didn't she know it was unsafe? Had no one told her? She appeared unaware of her danger and I opened my mouth to cry out a warning. Yet something stayed my tongue.

It was undoubtedly one of the servants who had escaped to this remote spot for a few minutes of privacy and rest, for no one was with her; she had come alone. Would it be dangerous to call out and perhaps startle her—should one speak softly? Surely she would have been alerted if the structure was that unsafe! How could I make her understand her danger, without precipitating the very thing I feared? If I dared warn her, whoever she was, and simply let it go at that, no one would know rules had been disobeyed. It was common knowledge that the Old House was closed to casual traffic—but possibly the girl would have disregarded that and come anyway.

The ritual of combing ended, the young woman laid down her brush and commenced to braid her long hair. The old boards creaked ominously, I could hear them.

"Please," I called fearfully, "please—don't be alarmed—" But the figure didn't turn, the girl hadn't heard me. I stepped nearer, having first to move around some large couch or armchair sheeted for protection, and when I looked up the girl was gone. Hairbrush and figure had vanished, the chair was empty, there was only the late bright sunshine on the loose boards where she had been sitting.

There must be another exit that had allowed her to slip unobserved into some connecting room, and away. It was understandable; she had simply feared to acknowledge my reminder and left. But how had she moved so silently? Examination did reveal another door, a small one leading into the garderobe, and it was ajar. I sighed with relief. So the young woman had retreated, and safely. There would be a way to learn from Madame or from someone on the household staff whether or not sufficient warning had been issued so all understood. Otherwise, having no wish to get the girl into trouble, I would not speak of it.

Glancing at my pendant watch I was surprised to see that it was near dinnertime. I went back the same route I had come, aware of just how little ground I had covered in almost two hours. As I passed through the huge banquet hall

there was again the deep, clutching silence—the silence of
the dead, echoing only to my own footsteps. Again nearing
the *directrice's* territory, I found no one in sight.

"What did you do?" Madame asked the next morning.
She appeared to be in high spirits. A vase of fresh violets
stood on the little sideboard though it was not yet eight
o'clock, and the metal box I had observed before reposed,
with its lid carefully shut, upon a chair. I thought Jason
might have brought the violets.

Not mentioning my encounter with Divino, I explained.
"I saw the solar. It is old, and precious—a glimpse into life
as people lived it long ago. The privy was boarded up as you
said. I saw the balcony too, but didn't go out on it, of course.
Is it very dangerous?"

The old lady glanced at me quickly. "Yes. It is. Why?"

I hesitated. "I was just wondering if everybody knew
about it. Do any of the servants, or guests from this side,
ever go over there? I was thinking if the warning had not
been heeded someone could take a nasty fall. It did seem to
me a great drop from that balcony. I wouldn't care to
venture out upon it."

Madame was for a moment deeply thoughtful. "Everyone knows," she asserted. "No one goes into the Old House
without express permission from me. I knew you would
respect its heritage value; I also knew you would obey my
warnings. Others might not do so. That balcony is definitely
not safe. If you saw someone out on it—did you see
someone on it?"

The question was unexpected and I couldn't lie. The old
lady must have read her answer from my expression. "Long
flowered robe, red brocade slippers? Black hair. She's been
combing her hair on that balcony for over a hundred years.
What you saw was a ghost."

I could not have been more shocked. "But it was a living
person! I saw her with my own eyes—!"

"Of course you did. Though no one else has for—let me
see—fifty years at least. I saw her once when I was a young
widow but it didn't frighten me; I'd been warned. I'd even
been told her name, Mathilda Manona, dubbed Nona, the

second Nona, that is, a descendant of that rascal upstairs. It was his doing, that black hair. Did you see her face?''

I was still shaken. So this was how other people must feel when they saw ghosts! It was my lot in life to see apparitions; I shouldn't be upset at this one. ''No,'' I said, ''she didn't turn toward me at all.''

''Just seeing her is supposed to be good fortune. Were you frightened?''

''No,'' I said again, ''I didn't know she wasn't real. I spoke to her and tried to tell her of her danger but I thought she didn't hear. Before I could call again she'd gone, slipped through the garderobe door without my noticing.''

The old lady nodded. ''So she would. So she has always done. She's a ghost, all right. You saw nothing else?''

''No, was I supposed to?''

Madame laughed heartily at that. ''Not necessarily, but the banqueting hall is said to be peopled with shadows— spirits, I mean. I've never seen any, but sounds can be heard quite frequently—activity, echoes, voices, or so it has been reported. It seems we have an old den of ghosts here, but none so far have bothered me, and what is more important, none have bothered my guests.'' She tipped her head and gazed at me through half-closed eyes. ''Fifty years, and you're here a little over a month and make her acquaintance. Are you sure you're not on speaking terms with spooks?''

It was lightly said and meant nothing, but I was glad when the old lady nodded to the box on the chair. ''Get that for me, will you, and lock it in the safe again? I've found what I want out of it for now. My memory box,'' she said.

All she had left of family? Pity struck me. I did as I was asked and explained further what I had seen in the old section. ''Part of it was fine and appeared to be sound and in good shape, but the other part didn't look as if anything had been done to it at all.''

''Precious little!'' the old lady snorted. ''I'm just too stubborn to give up, I guess.''

''How many rooms do you have?''

''Over there, you mean? On the south side, sixteen on the first floor. Twenty, counting the breakfast rooms. No adequate plumbing, lighting, or heating, only fireplaces, candles, and solars.''

And what use would the bodiless have for plumbing, lighting, or heating? Because I hadn't heard anything yesterday didn't mean they weren't there. Yvonne would be with them. I would have liked to ask about Yvonne but looked at the old lady and decided not to. It could stir up a barrage of questions.

''I should mention too that there are no coverings at all on the furniture in the West Banquet Hall, or on the armor. Even the armorial bearings and all the banners are in place.''

Madame frowned. ''I suppose I should drop the restoration,'' she said. After a silence, she added, ''No, I won't! So help me I'll have Latham and Bennett look at it—they're the best contractors in Montreal. Couldn't get them before, maybe we can now. Make a note of it, will you?''

That same afternoon a representative of the firm arrived and looked the job over; they would come shortly to begin work. Madame Crecy was elated; she couldn't believe that at last she would have what she wanted.

Little remained of the day, and somewhat short of four o'clock she pushed aside her books and flexed her fingers. I had been transposing notes with Madame's guidance.

''I'm tired. Not many hours put in, but much ground covered. Will you be dining in the dining room tonight?''

''I'd thought to, yes. Why? Did you need me for something?''

''No, nothing like that. I was going to ask you to have dinner here with me but if you have other plans—We could go down into the garden sometime, if you like. It need not wait for company.''

Lonely? She wanted me around a little longer? I smiled. ''We could go now, if you want to.''

''No,'' she said, and sighed. ''I think I'm just weary, that's all. Jason came with another problem—but no matter, you run along. I'll see you in the morning.''

I watched a moment; she'd swung back to the desk, and with purpose was already lifting a ledger from a drawer. I was fairly certain I knew what was on her mind—the extensions for the tenants' garden that Jason was opposing. He'd opposed projects before, strongly, and Madame knew her own mind and precisely what she wanted. She'd hold out, but that was not to say that the disagreements didn't tire her.

Whose money was it after all? Shouldn't she be allowed to spend it any way she liked? I wondered whether Jason cared for Crecy itself, or only for its worth, what it meant in dollars and cents. Was evaluation—his own word—the yardstick by which he measured the Château? With a stab of annoyance I thought, if Divino was the eyes and ears of this place, Jason was its purse strings.

I was glad he was not in the dining room that night; though it was none of my business at all, I would have been hard put to keep a bridle on my tongue.

I ate my meal grimly, and presently became aware of the little old lady at the next table, watching me. I smiled, she dimpled, and then as if surprised at her own boldness, she rose and carefully carried her teacup to my table.

"May I?"

"Of course! Please do." I sprang to pull out a chair for her and we sat companionably opposite one another.

"We have not seen very much of you," she offered in her crackly voice, "you are always so busy running to and fro. But we thought we knew who you were. It is so nice to have a young person at the Château—you are Miss Kirkwood, are you not? I heard someone say."

"Yes," I replied gravely, "and it is very nice to know you."

She was Miss Fortescue, a maiden lady, originally from England but living in Canada these many years. Wasn't this a lovely place? She was so happy here.

The conversation progressed to the weather, the excellence of the food at Crecy, the beauty and comfort of the surroundings. We got on wonderfully; she was sweet and kind and I very much enjoyed talking to her. Up until now they had been only a sea of faces, these guests of Madame's. Now I was working for them as well. I had often wondered about the guests, but respected their privacy as individuals. I knew that this exchange would be remembered and discussed among them for some time to come.

After the meal was over I went up to my quarters, read a while, bathed, and went to bed early. But I slept badly that night. Through my dreams I seemed to hear a persistent voice, a voice that whispered, *Be careful of those stairs. Be—careful—of—those—stairs—*

I woke with a start, but there was no one in the room with me; I was alone. The suite was utterly still. Bright moonlight streamed through the curtains and lay in broad bars across the bed.

Stairs? What stairs? My sleep-fogged brain fumbled at the words. Symbolic? Or imagination? More likely it was the tag end of a dream, and the words meant nothing.

I lay quietly and after a while dozed a bit, then suddenly I jerked awake at a sound outside the door. I stiffened, trying to identify the sound, but all I could hear was the muffled thump of my own heart. Again—it came again, the swish of a foot on carpet. I raised up on an elbow and stared in strange fascination at the door. Slowly the knob moved; I could see it gleaming clearly in the moonlight. Again very slowly the knob turned, then eased back to its former position as the unseen hand outside the door released it. I exhaled my breath in a long sigh; I hadn't known I was holding it. Swiftly I got out of bed and crossed the room to the door and pressed my ear to the panel. There was the faint sound of a departing footfall, the rustle of garments as if the would-be intruder wore long skirts. Then silence. I returned to bed, but not to sleep.

Who was it? Who in the household would come to my room in such fashion? I had been at Crecy long enough for the help to be aware of the location of my suite. What the person—and I was certain it was a woman—would have done had she decided to enter, I had no way of knowing. At any rate, I assured myself shakily, hereafter I would wedge a chairback firmly beneath the knob of the door when I retired.

And what about the warning I had heard? I'd thought of

Yvonne, but it was not Yvonne. The girl would have shown herself. Be careful of what stairs? I didn't have the slightest notion what the words referred to—there were stairs all over the place, but why was it necessary to be warned against them?

CHAPTER 9

I awoke listless and depressed, but after splashing cold
water on my face and taking ample time to ready myself
before going downstairs, I felt better.

The morning began with a departure from routine. It
seemed that stronger lighting had been ordered for the small
gallery, and Madame wanted to know if the changes had
been accomplished satisfactorily. I'd left Jason with her,
discussing a certain picture in the gallery upstairs—the
damned thing wouldn't stay hung, I'd heard Jason say as I
left. I suppose he referred to the large one I'd seen with its
face turned to the wall. Jason was leaving shortly, then
Madame had a man coming in with some carpet samples she
wanted to see, so I was to take my time.

Certainly everything was perfect here. I looked around
the room appreciatively. The newly refinished floor glowed
with a beautiful luster; the lighting was just right to show
the masterpieces to the very best advantage. I saw all the
precious works I had expected—Degas; Sargent; a gentle
country scene glimmering with unbelievable brilliance.

But the awareness that it was Friday, and the end of the
week, urged me downstairs. I was reading in the lounge
when Albert was announced.

I rose as he came forward to greet me, holding out his
hands, and this time I placed mine within them with no
hesitation at all.

"It is good to see you," he said quietly.

"And to see you. Would you like to sit down?" Then I remembered Madame's offer. "Or there is a place where we can go to chat, if you like. It's just out beside the house, quite lovely and considerably cooler than in here."

We turned in this direction and I caught a wave from above; it was Madame Crecy on the balcony.

"It seems someone wants to get your attention," Albert remarked with a smile. "Your employer?"

"Yes," I said, "come. You can meet her." Together we climbed the stairs. I made the presentation, Albert replying with a gracious bow, and I saw the old lady's eyes light up with appreciation at the courtesy.

"Madame Crecy? A very great honor," he murmured.

I heard her reply, "Mr. St. Denis, this is a happy day and the pleasure is mine." Then her eyes twinkled, and she said gravely, "Perhaps Paulette has mentioned my private garden. You two young people are welcome to enjoy it—the house is yours."

"A very grand lady," my companion said as we returned downstairs, then through the door and out into the bright sunshine.

"Yes," I agreed, "she is," remembering that I had once said those exact words myself.

We found a stone bench and sat down, and sudden and painful silence descended. I groped for words to say— something, anything to bridge the awkward moment.

"How have you been?" we said simultaneously, then looked at each other and burst into laughter. But almost at once he became serious. "Truly—how have you been faring? Is the position working out as well as you hoped?"

I looked down at my hands; feeling him so near I had an almost irresistible urge to reach out and touch him, for him to touch me. "Better," I said, "even much better. It is a wonderful place, a wonderful position, and Madame Crecy is—well, one of a kind and all you think she might be. She has a sense of humor; she can laugh. She's direct, and kind."

"I gathered that. And on the debit side?"

"You mean . . . problems?" I hesitated, but with him I could be honest. I would be frank without going into detail. I mentioned the difficulty the old lady had been having with her manager, that all was not well there.

As though he sensed my reservation he asked bluntly, "And what about you? Does any of this extend to you?"

"It can make things unpleasant," I admitted, "but it is Madame Crecy I worry about."

"I see," Albert said, and again, "I see." Then, "And the other considerations?"

I shook my head and now smiled freely. "I've met them, one at any rate. Her name is Yvonne. It sounds crazy, but her name is Yvonne."

Once again he hadn't long; we talked for a while, filling in bits of our personal history from those missing years so each knew the other much better than before. He wished he had time to see some of the house himself, he said. He had always been fascinated by old homes, and this one seemed to be unique—one of a kind. And so long as I was happy here, I could handle anything that came along. If he were nearer—but as he'd said before, this assignment might take some time.

At last he stood up to go; I thought if he opened his arms I would have fallen into them.

He stood facing me, his eyes searching my face, touching my lips. "I wouldn't have left without seeing you again," he said. "I haven't been able to get you out of my mind. Even back in school I was drawn to you but afraid to admit it."

"Because I was different."

"Yes, and I regret that foolishness, and the time wasted. Paulette," he asked huskily, "is there someone else?"

My throat was full, the word came with difficulty. "No." And knew it to be true.

"I'll be back, will you wait for me? I'll send you my address. Will you write?" I nodded yes. Before he left, his hands touched my shoulders, and he leaned down and very gently brushed my lips with his own. Walking slowly from the garden, I wanted to cry. That brief touch, that tiny moment of bliss had to last until he returned. It was a promise; I would wait. There were many things I didn't say that he probably wanted to ask about, but he would write and I'd answer; there would be that bridge of letters between us.

I had been so totally unaware of our surroundings, it was as though I hadn't seen the garden at all. And it was hard to return to the prosaic world of ledgers and journals and papers to file. Looking back on it I think Madame must have made it easy for me, for I cannot remember that much was accomplished. At two we had tea, at three she laid down her pen and announced that I was free to go; she had some notes to sign and then she, too, was quitting for the day. We would get an early start tomorrow. In the meantime, if I did any roaming, I was to remember that she always appreciated reports of what I saw.

If she only knew how many things I couldn't tell her! There were those, the lucky ones, whose second sight disappeared sometime early in life; one of my aunts lost hers in puberty, another with marriage, a great-uncle before he was twenty. I had long hoped that by some miracle I, too, would be freed, but such was not the case. Always I feared discovery, and when the old lady came upon me unexpectedly in the hall later that afternoon, I was almost lost. For as I was thinking of Yvonne, Yvonne appeared.

The second-floor windows at Château Crecy were set deeply into the casements, the walls thick—possibly as a protective measure in hazardous times past—and each window, thus positioned into the walls, boasted its ample window ledge. I was sitting on the ledge and remained so quietly for a time, enjoying the warmth of the sunshine on my shoulders and savoring the silence and peace of the great house. Dreaming quietly, I became aware of a drifting chill as though storm clouds had gathered, and there was the sound of rushing wind.

The clatter of coach wheels on cobbles and the restless prancing of horses. They pulled up before a porte cochere, the door opened and people began getting out. There was

*talk and laughter, the murmur of ladies and the louder
voices of the men.*

"Limpole Road?"

"Oh, no!" The door slammed. "Drive on!"

"At once, Your Grace!"

I looked up and saw Yvonne, and this time there was no
shock at all, no surprise. "Do you always come where I
am?"

"You do not wish me to?" The girl spoke with gentle
reproof; she seemed older and sadder than before.

I shook my head. "It doesn't matter." I glanced up and
down the long hall; it was empty.

"My baby died, you know. Poor little baby, poor little
son. His name was Roger. He breathed twice and died.
Mathilda said I had cursed him, but it was not so, it was not
so! I would have lived for him but they wouldn't let me. If
anyone were guilty of cursing it was Thomas. He was a
devil, that Thomas! God's death! how she hated him. She
hated everyone. That is why she spoke ill of me, but 'twas
not because of that my baby died but because I was so
small—the veriest child. I am not a child now," she added
simply. "I would ha' loved him."

"Ah," I breathed, feeling suddenly sorry for this small
unhappy wraith who was so like myself. I leaned my head
back against the window casing and closed my eyes.

"Would you want me to go?"

"No," I murmured. "Can't you forget, about the baby, I
mean? I know that it was a long time ago."

"Aye. You are right. What's done is done and cannot be
undone. You have been here such a short while and already
you think to go away?"

I opened my eyes, startled. "Why—yes. It is true.
Sometimes I wonder if it wouldn't have been better for all
of us if I hadn't come."

"You could not help yourself for coming. It was not of
your own will. But that is something you already know. Yet
sometimes I am surprised—it seems so long."

"What seems so long?"

"That you should not understand and believe. Remember

I said once all would be well, did I not? But you fear—oh
so many things—'' The girl broke off, shrugged again. She
spoke, then, of her past life, where she had been and what
she had done, rapidly and clearly and without pause as
though expecting no reply. And having little curiosity left as
to the whys and wherefores of these things and as a result
having abandoned any disbelief, I simply listened. I failed to
hear Madame as the wheelchair rolled up quietly on the
deep carpet.

''What were you looking at?''

I froze. ''Why, I—nothing, Madame! Nothing, of course.
There is a view from here.''

''I see. The Old House. Yes. A part of it. The Tower and
the South Wing. The balcony, too, a bit of it. And the
courtyard.''

Full of desperation I said, ''Yes, all of that. I was on my
way to my room and saw it. Did you want me?''

''No. But I wondered about you. And when I come upon
you staring at an empty space I wonder still more. What do
you see that none of the rest of us can see? Paulette, are
you—psychic?''

''Why?'' I cried bitterly. I was trembling; fear got in my
throat and in my voice. ''Just because I sit quietly and
daydream?'' My face was stiff from trying to contain my
emotions. All I wanted was to get away! But the girl was
gone—the girl was gone. For Madame she'd never been. ''I
often do that,'' I said in a gentler tone, ''I'm sorry if you
were concerned. May I go now?''

''You may go now,'' Madame agreed and spread her
hands in defeat.

The old lady felt puzzled and hurt, I knew, but I couldn't
help myself. How could I tell her about the Château's
inmate, explaining that the girl wore blue today, that she had
tiny feet, that I was absolutely certain now, without a
shadow of a doubt, who she was? Yvonne de Cheltenham,
dead of childbed fever? Paris, 1640. Her mother was a
Spieret, of Avignon—an ancestor of mine. Then, for the
first time, it occurred to me that if it happened again, if
Madame brought up the subject and I got up enough

courage, might I not speak of what ailed me? But the courage was not mine now.

No mention was made of the incident, and work went on as usual. Another afternoon, having finished several letters, Madame said she was tired and wished her dinner early. I was to complete what remained of the correspondence the next morning. There was no rush anyway, she told me. She'd get Divino up here with some hot tea; she could use it. Jason came in and spoke to her, and turning almost lazily, enveloped me in a caressing glance.

"Won't you please put this back where it belongs?" the old lady asked me and reached into a drawer of her desk. "Don't bother with it now. Keep it in your room overnight, just return it to the case in the morning."

I stared. "But isn't this Manona—the second image we spoke about?"

The old lady nodded. The black hair on the doll was brushed satin-smooth and lay decorously beneath the head-dress of heavy lacquer red satin and jewels, which fell from the regal little head to the hem of the long robe. The face was indistinct but the tiny lips were primly pursed; no emotion at all disturbed the grotesquely white-painted cheeks. Jason carried the doll to the window, examining it.

"And to think she killed her husband. Wouldn't believe it to look at her, would you?" He came back and stood turning the slim exquisite thing over in his hands, then laid it on the desk, shaking his head.

"It would have been all right," Madame growled, "if Thomas could have kept his hands off the ladies. It was his undoing. The Chinese in Manona made her a deliberate adversary, cool under duress; the Polynesian, hot-blooded and reckless. She never forgave and she never forgot. It was the finish of a scoundrel but the finish of her as well. Nor did Nona trouble to profess her innocence; she'd done exactly as she meant to do. He'd been taken ill with an attack of fever and Nona nursed him as a dutiful wife should. She simply substituted a poisonous draught for the palliative prescribed. He died cursing her. And it's said she died cursing him, for she followed soon after, by the same method. A violent family." The old lady paused, looking idly at me. "The peacemakers, the quiet ones, came from outside. But I digress." She smiled.

I reached out and touched the dainty painted lips of the doll with a careful finger. Poor Manona. She didn't have a chance. Thomas had stormed through life and taken her with him. "There are about fifty of these, aren't there?"

Again the old lady nodded. "Fifty-six, good or bad. The male costume in each case is a badge of honor representing a service done by that individual to the country whose costume he wears."

"Why only fifty-six?"

"Thomas disliked many people," Madame said succinctly, "and most of the dolls show what he secretly thought of them by the way their features were exaggerated. For all that, he left us a fine collection."

"This doll alone must be worth a fortune," I commented. "How did it get down here?"

"I had it brought down," the old lady replied, "to have some repairs done. The headdress was loose."

"And you want me to take it to my room, and in the morning return it?" I repeated, remembering all the goings-on at that location of late. "I couldn't possibly, you know." I hesitated; I had become aware of a strangeness, an increasing sense of unreality, of something false. On the surface all appeared normal enough. Jason stood, back to us, looking out the window; he didn't turn. So he was involved, too. He knew something I didn't know; they both knew something.

Picking up the doll, I could feel again the rich fabric, the brocade gold-threaded and stiff with jewels under my fingers. "I shouldn't be so concerned," I said to the old lady, "but you see I have never handled anything so costly. I know what it means to you, what it would mean to me, particularly since it is an heirloom. No wonder the case is kept locked. I only thought—well, having it in my suite might not be such a good idea. I wouldn't want to be responsible. It is safer with you."

"Safer in the case." Madame laughed. "And you worry

too much. My dear, it is only a toy! Jason, ring for Hilda, will you? I've waited long enough for my tea.'' And to me, ''As you wish.'' She waved her hand carelessly. ''I only thought since the Trophy Room would take you considerably out of your way, you might as well wait until tomorrow, but if you'd feel easier in your mind, go now. Here—'' She pushed two keys on a small ring across the desk to me. ''At any rate, don't bother to bring the keys back; bring them in the morning.''

I took the ring and went out, returned the doll to the case, and closed and locked the case securely, and with the second key, the larger brass one, relocked the door after me. Then slowly I returned to my own quarters.

Why had Madame suddenly wanted to get rid of me? It was after I had examined the doll. And why had she wanted me to take the doll to my room, such a valuable object as that? Undoubtedly she did not share my opinion but in any case it was far too important to be treated so lightly. But had Madame thought she was treating it lightly? What was her motive?

Obviously Jason was in the office for a purpose; she'd wanted to talk to Jason. Why? Why had she wanted to talk to Jason in particular just then?

At this point I told myself I was being silly. There was not a reason in the world why I should feel the way I did. Anyway, I was making too much of it. I was merely an employee here, a friend of Madame's perhaps, but certainly not privileged to follow all her movements. Jason worked for her too, and business could be confidential. But I was shocked to realize just how proprietary my interest in the old lady had become, and I told myself firmly that working for the Mistress of Crecy gave me no rights beyond a paycheck. I should remember that I was no more than an employee in this place, and to conduct myself accordingly. Nothing gave me leave to watchdog her moves, to monitor her thoughts or to question her decisions. Yet a feeling of betrayal remained.

CHAPTER 10

❧

The next morning I unlocked and entered the office preparatory to taking up the duties of the day, something I
occasionally did when the old lady breakfasted downstairs
and lingered over her meal.

Shortly she appeared, and business went on as usual. But
her thoughts seemed elsewhere, and when in late afternoon
an abrupt knock sounded on the door she started almost
violently. Before I could answer the door it burst open in my
face. Hilda Divino stood there, two shrinking maids standing beside her—Cook's helpers, I knew them to be.

The *directrice* was livid with rage. It was the kitchens
again. They were a shambles. One of the girls stuttered in
her fear; she seemed unable to express herself at all. Mrs.
Divino, that dark, stern automaton, was the voluble one.

"I can't tell you what did it! Pots tumbled from hooks
and flew across the room; dishes fell from cupboards and
smashed on the floor."

Madame Crecy looked at her in disbelief. "Did you see
it yourself or are you just reporting? Were you actually
present when this took place?"

Mrs. Divino drew herself up; the black eyes shot fire. She
hadn't glanced in my direction; it was as though I didn't
exist. "Do you think I'm lying? Go see for yourself or ask
these girls here—if the stupid things can talk!"

"I intend to," Madame snapped. She said evenly,

"You've been here for years, looked over the maids' shoulders from cellars to attic, and now you can't keep things in order? Get hold of yourself! And you, Francie, stop sniveling! You'll get nowhere that way." Madame wheeled herself forward swiftly. "Now let's get to the bottom of this—what did *you* see?"

"Things b-broke," tearfully gurgled the one called Francie. "I think it is spirits. I ran! My father knew a man once who had the Evil Eye. I think she's got the Evil Eye!" Francie pointed at Divino. A thin blond girl, she trembled violently. It was clear she was completely terrified.

"Bosh." Madame snorted inelegantly. "When I see it I'll believe it. And you, Katrine, what's your version? Speak up, girl! Or did you run, too?"

The girl addressed shook her head. She'd seen it all. Katrine's story was virtually the same. It had been going on for some time, though not much at first so they didn't think anything of it. Only objects misplaced—a paring knife, a sieve, once a cutting-board, another time a stack of kitchen towels—and the girls were blamed. Later the towels were found scattered on the floor of the utility closet. She'd been frightened then and wanted to come tell Madame but the manager wouldn't let her. Even Katrine, dumpy and phlegmatic, was visibly upset, her eyes red from weeping.

"Why wouldn't you let her come tell me?"

"She had work to do!"

"Next time see to it that she is allowed to present her case to me in person! I have stressed this before and I mean to be obeyed! We will have no high-handed rule of that kind in my house. There has been entirely too much hullabaloo lately and I'm tired of it. What happened in the kitchens is merely the result of improper storage—kettles too carelessly hung upon hooks, dishes stacked too near shelf-edges. Now get out, all of you. I want peace and quiet."

The door closed much more softly than it had opened, and the hubbub retreated, then vanished altogether.

"What an uproar." Madame dropped her head wearily on her hands. "Sometimes I wonder how we are able to keep it from the tenants. And sometimes I wonder about Hilda!

She should be able to do better than this—she's had enough practice.'' She glanced at the clock; it was nearly four. ''We may as well call it a day,'' she said, and sighed. ''You haven't told me your opinion of this.''

I shook my head. ''I don't know that I should have one. But it has to be as you said, of course. Pots don't jump down off hooks by themselves.'' But going upstairs I added to myself, Any more than portraits climbed down from walls by themselves?

It was when I was changing before dinner that I remembered the keys. In my pocket—the keys to the Trophy Room and the collection case! Yes, they were there, I'd forgotten to give them to Madame. Hurriedly I completed dressing and left the room. What on earth would the old lady think?

I had reached Madame Crecy's door and almost opened it before I realized that Madame had a visitor. In the act of turning away I caught voices and stood, frozen.

''Do you think she suspects?''

''Of course not, I'll hold up my end.''

''All right. As for the other, my common sense tells me I'm crazy. Just one other possibility and I refuse to believe that. Not all the way from''—the words were blurred—''. . . I have to be sure. What's taking Sirios so long? Greece isn't that far away.''

''I wouldn't wait too long.''

The old lady grunted. ''Can't you see I need help? This house has to be cared for and properly run. I can't do it alone. When the time comes there'll be recompense enough, and that's all she cares about. Think I'm under any illusions there?''

Then, momentarily roused from my shock, I realized what I was doing. They had been discussing me. Jason? Jason and Madame. A conversation meant to be private. *An eavesdropper hears nothing good about himself.* Somewhere I'd read that. They seemed to be questioning my arrival here: But why should they, since I'd come as a stranger to them both, just as any other tourist capable of reading a guidebook or travel brochure? As for what Madame suspected, that I did not know. Utterly sick at heart

I returned to my quarters, to collect myself as best I could before returning to the office.

When I arrived there Jason had gone, and Madame's preoccupation provided good cover for my own reticence: I dropped the keys on the desk and the old lady absent-mindedly returned them to the drawer without question.

"Thank you," she said, only adding that she had trades-men coming shortly and I was free for the rest of the day. I murmured a reply and went out.

I avoided Jason that night, avoided everyone, not even going down to dinner. I didn't get much sleep either but by morning I was able to face the situation with some measure of calm. It was hard to believe a conspiracy existed between Madame and Jason; for what reason? I wasn't an important enough employee for that. As for the mention of recom-pense, did she actually think I'd come to Crecy for a purpose? Yet who knew what she thought? This was a wealthy house, I was virtually penniless; such things had been done before. What I'd overheard I considered sense-lessly cruel, because who could they have been talking about except me? There should be some warning system, I thought bitterly; this was twice now I'd eavesdropped.

That night Jason stopped me in the hall. "Where have you been? I have missed seeing you—eating alone is not very enjoyable." He eyed me anxiously. "Are you all right?"

"Oh, yes. Of course." I heard my voice with some surprise; it sounded natural. "I was just very tired, that was all. There have been more disturbances in the kitchens."

"I think I know who is at the bottom of the disturbances. Damn that woman," Jason muttered, then caught himself back. "Aren't you coming to dinner?"

I shook my head. "I don't think so. I had cocoa and a pastry earlier and that's all I want."

"What you need," he said, "is to get away from this place for a while. Get out, see something new and differ-ent."

He was probably right and I even admitted to myself that it did sound good—in my state of mind, it sounded particularly good. But I shook my head. Right now, I told him, I planned to read for a while and relax; there was a book I wanted to finish. He only nodded graciously and went his way.

Peace in the household was short-lived. The next day as I worked with Madame, Divino again appeared at the door, this time holding something behind her back, a look of triumph on her face as her eyes sought mine. *Now I've got you*, that look said. *Now I've got you where I want you, my girl. Try and get out of this!*

She plunked an object, broken and torn, on the desk before Madame. The old lady stared. "What's this?"

I gasped. It was the doll, the beautiful red and gold Manona doll, its clothing rumpled and torn, the headdress ripped. Two large rubies were missing from the headdress.

The old lady's face hardened. "Where did you get it?"

"From the floor outside her door. She had the keys; she kept them overnight. She is the only one who had them," the manager snarled. "I've never had this thing in my hands before and you know it. I don't hanker after such fripperies. But ask her."

"How do you know Paulette had the key?"

"I saw her with it!"

While my fortunes go up, hers go down, I thought, or was it the other way around? This woman was fighting for every inch of ground by fair means or foul. The black gaze again darted past Madame to me. She slyly asked, "You were supposed to lock up—why didn't you?"

The old lady seemed to shake herself free of her momentary shock. "That will be enough! As a matter of fact this doll was replaced in the case, the case and door both locked afterward."

"Then"—the manager's eyes slid to me again—"how does it happen that one of the maids saw her this morning with that very same doll?"

"Which maid?"

Divino didn't reply. There was an instant's swirling silence and once more Madame stepped into the breach. "You are mistaken," she said coldly. "Such a thing cannot be true. I now have the keys in my possession, safe. Paulette gave them back to me two days ago. Also, the toy is here now, and safe. I shall have it fixed. Do you have anything more to say?''

"I've said it," Divino stated grimly, and stalked out.

I stood by the window and stared down into the lovely garden dreaming in the noonday sun. The window was open and a breeze gently blew, rippling the surface of the pool; a robin chirped from the old maple beside the house. I came back to my chair and sat down; words formed on my lips but I cast them aside. I looked up at Madame Crecy as from a great distance. The old lady was waiting.

"I'll try to explain. I only know I took the doll as you told me to do and locked it in its case. I locked the door too, as you said. I came down to give you the keys—" I faltered, my fingers twisted in my lap, "but you were talking to Jason. It was—about me. I couldn't—come in then, so I went back to my room. The keys were in my pocket and I forgot they were there. I brought them back the next morning. And that's—all." I looked away miserably.

The old lady's voice broke the silence. "I understand."

"You do?"

"Of course. It never occurred to me not to believe you. This whole thing is a mistake. The doll is torn, and eventually I shall find out who did it. I'm sorry you overheard Jason's and my conversation; half-truths can be more damning than the whole could possibly be. However, I'm not in a position to discuss the matter right now. Suffice it to say that no wrong was directed at you personally—and I'd like you to believe that.''

Nothing the old lady could say, I thought gratefully, could have made me feel better.

Madame smiled and her face seemed to grow gentler. "Don't worry about it," she said lightly. "I've never known Hilda Divino to lie before, but I don't know. I still can't believe she took that doll. She says she found it in the hallway; I do not see how such a thing can be. We'll get that part of it straightened out sooner or later, too. As far as the kitchens are concerned, I believe it is all a tempest in a teapot. Careless cook, careless help, and things tumble onto the floor. That pots and pans single out Divino for assault, I cannot believe. She's always had a good imagination, and a good temper; she'll use any excuse to raise the roof with the help. Jealousy, I suspect. I see she is not above drawing you into it also; well, we'll see about that. She's not a bad person underneath, only sour. Her past life has embittered her toward everything and everybody. She'll simmer down."

"You're not angry with me?"

"Of course not."

"But you don't believe my story," I said slowly. "You are only trying to save my feelings."

The old lady sat silent a moment. "I'm going to tell you something," she said at last. "I don't want you to be shocked or frightened. The truth is, I don't think there is any mistake here at all. I think the supernatural is at work. All the evidence supports it. The why, now in particular, escapes me. I only hope it runs its course before it empties my house. I've kept roomers so long I'd be lost without them." She chuckled. "Pots and pans—is some ghost trying to be funny? A sense of humor, no doubt. Once in every donkey's years we should expect activity of the sort at Crecy—it keeps tradition alive, you know."

I stood up; on impulse I leaned and bestowed a kiss on her withered cheek. "Thank you for believing in me," I said, and went out.

But I was thinking hard. A portrait which refused to stay hung, pots and pans flying in the kitchens, objects that came up missing—the manager was at a loss to account for such phenomena. But I knew this type of wild activity sometimes occurred around the strong-tempered, because of strong emotions, and this, I was sure, was the reason here. There was no scientific explanation for it, but what scientific explanation was there for Thomas, or Manona, or Yvonne?

As I entered my quarters I stopped, startled, then flung up my head, sharply alert. Was it smoke I smelled?

Five rooms comprised the suite; the trouble was not in the sitting room—but hadn't I left that door open? I rushed to the bathroom but nothing was amiss there, so I returned hurriedly to my starting point. I ran to the bedroom and snatched the door open, then horrified, I jumped. The small gas heater had tipped forward, facedown, on the carpet. I rushed to throw open the windows, coughing, for fumes and smoke were thick in the room, then hurried for water to quench the smoldering carpet. In a short while it would have burst into open flame.

But the smoke? It seemed to be coming from somewhere else also. I whirled and raced from room to room, following the smell. Smoke seeped from beneath the closet door in my bedroom! I yanked it open then reeled back, struck in the face by a smothering billow of acrid smoke. My clothing was on fire! On the floor, directly beneath a rack, a pile of rags smoldered, little tongues of flame licking upward. Disregarding the flames, I kicked the pile apart frantically then rushed to the bathroom for more water. Moments later, panting and disheveled and streaked with soot, I stood back to survey the damage. The fire was out and the floor around what was left of the sodden heap of rags was completely drenched with water. Three of my dresses were ruined, as was a pair of shoes; a traveling bag had been scorched and blackened at one end. In the bedroom, near where the heater had stood, lay a vase that had been used to quench the smolder in the carpet.

I pushed back the hair clinging damply to my forehead. *How* had this happened? In my suite, with its northern exposure, a heater was supplied for quick warmth on chilly mornings; perfectly safe, I'd used it before, but not this morning nor for several mornings.

Could a gust of wind have blown the curtain against a vase, tipped the vase off the table onto the heater, knocking it over? To my knowledge, there had been no wind. I picked up the vase and stared at it, then set it down slowly. Such a thing was remotely possible.

Cleaning up wouldn't be easy, and I'd have to do something about my dresses; I had barely enough to cover my needs as it was. I didn't know about the heater—that might have happened the way I thought—but not the rags in the closet. Where had they come from? Rags weren't combustible in themselves. Whose hands had struck the match? Someone who felt reasonably certain that the incident would not be reported to Madame. Who would know that I would see to protect the Mistress of Crecy?

Divino! So, I told myself, this was war. She hated me, for whatever reason had been conjured up by her twisted mind, and would do anything to get me out of here. Perhaps the first pile of rags had not been left by the maids, as I had believed. Had the perpetrator been frightened off, that time, before she could properly light the fire? I'd not thought to look for matches.

After the incident of the doll I was eager to blame Divino. My anger boiled over and I wanted to hunt the woman down then and there and throw the accusation in her face. But could I prove it? She would rave and deny my accusation. No, even as serious as this was, I wouldn't wait and watch. Once again I'd not carry tales to Madame; I knew what she'd been going through lately. If she heard of this, it would not be from me.

CHAPTER 11

"You look like a young lady of grim determination," Madame said the next morning when I looked up from my invoices.

"I hadn't known it showed." I managed a light laugh. The one thing I was sure did show was my lack of sleep.

"Anything I should know?" The old lady's glance was very keen.

"No, not really. I was thinking about buying a new dress or two, that's all. A trip to the city—"

No need to go to that bother, Madame said, there was a seamstress here at Crecy and she did beautiful work. Give her an idea of what I wanted, she urged, bolts of material would be sent, I could make my choices and the seamstress would get right to it.

Fortunately, coinciding with my need for the garments was an increase in salary, the old lady remarking it was scandalous that she paid her personal help less than she paid her cook. Henceforth and starting immediately, she said, my wages would be raised substantially. I blinked at the figure named, which seemed to me considerably more than substantial, but she waved away my thanks. I earned it, she said firmly, and more.

The renovation going on in the Old Wing was hardly noticed in the tenanted part of the Château. The mansion was so vast, the activity so far removed from the main part

102

of the house, that the construction was of no concern to the aged ones.

I immersed myself in my work; a week, two weeks passed. I'd not heard from Albert, but hardly expected to do so; I knew he must be busy and would write as soon as he could. I carried the thought of him constantly in my heart, how he walked, how he talked, that last precious touch of his lips against mine. Was he thinking the same of me? He had asked me to wait and I told him I would, with all that the promise implied.

I met the lady who could do marvelous things with a needle—the seamstress's name, appropriately enough, was Mrs. Able. She was a plump, cheerful, and energetic little person whose advice and counsel were most helpful. The material came, my choices were made, and fittings were arranged.

After a particularly busy period Madame insisted I take time off. "You're doing a marvelous job," the old lady said warmly. "I have some accounts to go over, so you are free. First, though, I have an errand for you. Check on the workmen in the Old Wing for me, see if they need anything, how the atmosphere is over there. If something is pressing come back and let me know."

I would be her emissary, I thought, and the responsibility pleased me. It pleased me too that under Madame's direction I had been allowed to take over many of the lesser, though still important, duties of running the Château. I enjoyed the responsibility, and for the first time in my life I felt truly a part of something.

As I was thinking these thoughts, I stopped stock-still in the long hallway as a figure came charging toward me: Thomas of Crecy—shiny boots, velvet trousers, and all—his voice a roar. I would have recognized him anywhere!

"Do we have to submit to this ripping and tearing? This is my home—can't the devils leave anything alone?" He banged his sword furiously on the floor. "Look at it—never the same again! Can't you put a stop to it?"

I'd thought sooner or later I would meet him, that he must be around somewhere. Now he had come as Yvonne had done and stood before me, spraddle-legged, furious. I could even speak to him as I did to Yvonne.

"It's because they *do* want to keep it the same that the work is going on. It's Madame Crecy's idea."

"Do *you* want it done?" He tipped his head and eyed me almost as if he were eager for my answer, as if it mattered what I thought.

"Yes, I would! How else can you keep timbers from falling down? The whole place from falling to pieces? Madame loves it."

"Madame—Madame—forget Madame!" Thomas said testily. "It doesn't matter, it's not hers anyway."

I could have argued the point, but didn't. Crecy was his and that was all there was to it. The scene had its more than ridiculous aspect. Suddenly Thomas gave me a stirred glance, melted into the air, and disappeared.

It seemed prudent to let the matter end there. Certainly this was one conversation I wouldn't report to Madame.

At the building site I found everything progressing well, all in order and no complaints, save for one man, a foreman, who came up to me as I was leaving.

"Who's the old boy in the funny costume?" he wanted to know. "I saw him and tried to climb down to where he was—I was out on that stringer there," he said, pointing. "But before I could get to him he took off. Figured if he didn't have anything important enough to say to stay around for, I wasn't going to worry."

I nodded solemnly. "You did exactly right. I don't think he'll be bothering you anymore," I said, imagining the reaction if they had known who the "old boy" actually was.

After reporting to Madame, I amused myself in the library until lunchtime. Jason found me in the dining room. "I never know whether you will be here or not," he complained as he pulled out a chair and seated himself. "I haven't seen much of you lately."

"It's true," I said lightly. "I've been busy and I suppose you have, too."

"Yes, it comes and goes." He attacked his salad with vigor, then looked up, his face grim. "There is something

I've meant to mention before and it's been on my mind, so I might as well bring it up. Has *Maman* warned you about Hilda Divino? I want you to know I'm on your side. Hilda is a troublemaker and has numerous ways of stirring things up. In spite of being only a servant in the place, she means to run everything, have everybody under her thumb. I wondered if you'd had any trouble with her yet.''

I hesitated. Instead of answering directly I said, ''Madame has had some brushes with her, yes.''

Jason took a sip of his coffee and pushed the cup back. ''Naturally,'' he said. ''It takes a strong-willed individual to withstand vitriol. *Maman* is strong but not invincible and if the day comes when she goes to pieces, Hilda will be to blame. I can't understand why she refuses to let Hilda go.'' Jason said this with resigned bitterness.

He told me that Madame's will stated that after she died the entire estate, save for gratuities to the other servants, would go to the manager.

''I warned her about leaving it all to one person,'' Jason added. ''Not that I think anything will happen, but I'd be better pleased if she'd leave it to a refuge for homeless cats.'' He said bluntly, ''When Hilda came here with her hard-luck story she knew she would find a solid berth and a cushy future. She knew what she was doing, that's what makes me so furious.''

Again I was surprised at his vehemence, but all I could say was that Madame must know her own mind.

''One can only hope,'' he said shortly. ''Still—'' He left the sentence hanging and glanced hastily at his watch. ''Whew, I have to run! I'm due in Court this afternoon and have barely enough time to make it.'' He paused and gave a wry smile. ''This has hardly been suitable lunchtime conversation for a lovely young lady, has it? When I could have been enjoying her company and listening to her interesting conversation. Perhaps later?'' Lifting his hand in salute, he was gone.

I rose and moved slowly out of the room. He had told me nothing I hadn't already known, or guessed. The information about the will was no surprise, nor that he resented

Divino. This new outburst could be merely the aftermath of the ongoing dissension between him and the manager. Yesterday morning I'd seated myself at a table near the entrance, almost at once I'd seen Jason and Divino locked in verbal combat by the far door. I had no idea what he might have said to her before my arrival, but I couldn't help hearing her shout—the whole dining room heard, though fortunately few tenants were present.

Mrs. Divino stood with her feet planted apart, her face a dark red. "You can't fire me, mister!" she'd yelled. "You've got no right—" Then she'd caught sight of me and her lips clamped shut. Jason's reply had been lost; he'd swung sharply on his heel and strode away. Had he purposely attempted to draw me out today, meaning to use my testimony against Divino with Madame? I was glad I had been evasive. I'd not carried tales to her so far, I certainly did not intend to do so through him.

Even before reaching the office I knew there was trouble today. Divino, never careful to keep her voice down, was shouting. She had been summoned by Madame and was being dealt with severely. I turned away but not soon enough. The door crashed open and the manager raced past like an avenging whirlwind, leaving the familiar stench in her wake. A dozen paces past me, she whirled to send me a vindictive glare, her lips moving with deadly invective. Then she stormed on her way. The entire scene sent chills down my back.

What I didn't understand I thought as I entered the office, was why, now, I was able to see so clearly the aura of blood-red haze that shimmered around her. What had been barely discernible before had grown until her body was completely encased in it. It moved with her when she moved; it stopped when she stopped. Rarely had I seen this and never, at any time, an aura of enough density not only to envelop the figure but very nearly obscure it.

How far would hatred push her? Other than the encounter with Marie—and that was confined to the kitchens—there had so far been no actual physical violence.

From Madame's standpoint the current situation was well

in hand. Divino had discharged a girl without permission and Madame had promptly hired her back.

"Hilda can't do that," Madame stated. "I won't have it! She knows better. Darcy is one of my best workers. She was trained in my kitchens and I expect to keep her for a good many years. For the life of me, I can't understand what's come over that woman! I'd like to know what really happened but Darcy won't say and I can't get anything out of Hilda."

I had my own clash with the manager a few days later. Trying hard to stay out of trouble, I ran full tilt into it. I literally bumped into Mrs. Divino, meeting her face to face. The tray the manager was carrying clattered to the carpet, teapot and tea things atop it. It was at the juncture of a corner, neither of us saw the other coming; the result was disastrous.

"I'm sorry!" I said at once as I would have said to anyone I'd nearly upset. "Here, let me help—" I knelt to gather the articles. Then I became aware that the woman had stepped deliberately forward, stood directly over me. Holding a fragile cup in my hand, I looked up.

"Leave them alone," Mrs. Divino ordered and remained towering above me. On her face was a clear look of superiority, and she was relishing my discomfiture. "Take your hands off those things," she repeated and stepped back. "We have servants for such chores. Or are you a servant?"

Slowly I rose from my knees. Unconsciously I'd relinquished the cup as I was bidden. Mrs. Divino's look held me; her words were flung with precision.

"You are a clumsy fool. Why don't you look where you're going? Banging around corners with no thought for anyone's safety!"

It was far and beyond a reaction fitting the deed and I bit my lips to keep from flinging back a sharp retort. No matter what I said, I realized, the result would have been the same. "I told you I was sorry," I said and was surprised at the calm I felt. "I offered to pick up the things." I added, "It wasn't my fault any more than it was yours, if you remember. We bumped into each other.''

The manager's stare never wavered. Nothing, I noted with relief, had been broken; all that happened was that the jam-pot spilled and the sticky mess was dribbled over everything. Madame had some lovely pieces and she would hate to have them destroyed.

''Next time you go sneaking around corners—''

Calm fled; I had the sudden impulse to reach out and throttle the creature. It shocked me and I said in even more careful tones, ''All right, fine, you say a servant should clean it up. We won't quarrel about that. But I want to make it clear I wasn't sneaking. How can you say such a thing? I'm told I have as much right in this house as you. I am not the interloper you seem to think I am. I have my duties to perform, work I am expected to do and get paid for, the same as any hired laborer. If you have complaints about me I suggest you lay them before Madame Crecy, as I have been asked to do, with mine.''

The black eyes widened at the unexpected rebuttal then narrowed, fastening upon me. The aura, now blood-red and terrifying in shape, was shifting, melting, reforming before my astonished gaze. It had the rank odor too—rank and identifiable. Now the aura was like a wall keeping me at arm's length; I thought if I touched it, it would burn.

''And you may go straight to the Devil! You mealy-mouthed upstart, ingratiating yourself with Madame, worming your way into this household, taking over—''

''Taking *over*?'' Patience was at an end; courtesy wouldn't work, politeness wouldn't. Hot anger swept through me, along with the uncontrollable urge to give back to this woman, with interest, all I had taken. I straightened sharply, facing her. If it was war, let it be a good one.

''So you don't like me, that's clear enough. Well, I'll tell you something. I don't like you either, so we're even. You've hated me from the start. But don't think you can drive me out, because it won't work.''

''I don't know what you're talking about!''

''Oh yes, I think you do. And incidentally, how good are

you at setting fires?'' I watched for the woman's reaction, and knew I'd struck home.

Divino's jaw clenched; sparks almost seemed to shoot from her eyes but guilt was written all over her. ''You dare—you dare—''

''I do, and more! After this, stay out of my rooms, understand? If you have business with me let it come through Madame, or say what you have to say straight to my face. And we'd both better keep out of each other's way, because from now on it won't be all one-sided. I belong here and so long as Madame Crecy is satisfied with my work, I am *staying*.'' Without another word I swung on my heel and walked away. At the door of my suite I turned and beheld my adversary still standing there; on her face was such a look of malevolent hatred it almost seemed to telegraph a curse to me. Then the aura again shifted and her figure was completely blotted out.

CHAPTER 12

❧

I hadn't heard from Albert, and the weeks had passed. I thought he must surely have reached his destination; he could have written if he'd wanted to. Couldn't he? Even a few lines, something to cling to, to warm my hands over, to renew myself. In my thoughts I penned cheerful, chatty little replies, all the while desperately missing him, for I knew now how deeply and completely I loved him. Yet each day there was no word—nothing.

I told myself I was being unduly concerned. He *would* write, but he had his duties, perhaps he had not found things quite as he expected upon his arrival. I tried to picture the place—the stark brightness of sun against baked red earth, the sounds of speech foreign to the ears, the smell of dust, of strange fruits— My best recourse, I knew, was to keep busy.

Jason hovered about, persistent in his attentions, still exhibiting the thoughtfulness and consideration of manner that had quite surprised me before. But sometimes even this became annoying. He brought me innumerable bouquets of flowers; they were left on the table in the dining room where I usually sat, or given to the maids to be presented to me as I entered.

"I wish you wouldn't," I protested when I again found flowers at my usual table.

"But why not? How else can a man show his feelings for

a young woman? Paulette, you must know how much I admire you! Dash it all—you make it difficult. Frankly, I wanted to ask if you would—''

We climbed the stairs to Madame's second floor; I was about to hear a declaration, and I was startled. He made as if to pull me around but I stepped aside, smiling lightly.

''You are always so elusive—! Well, what I wanted to say was, would you like to go for a drive sometime?''

''Oh,'' I said. ''Why—that might be nice.''

''Then perhaps we can make it soon—?''

I was spared the need for an answer. Madame's door opened and Divino emerged. She looked around me and spoke to Jason. ''Madame Crecy wants to see you.''

''I know that,'' he replied shortly, then he turned to me. ''This may take some time and I have an appointment this afternoon. Will I see you at breakfast tomorrow?''

''She's waiting!'' Divino growled and, without a backward glance, walked away.

I was happy enough to go the opposite direction without giving Jason an answer. I went down the long hallway then climbed the stairs, traversed another hallway and turned right, to the Old Wing. There I stood, looking and listening. The place was dead. Deserted. There were no echoes of activity; no life sounded anywhere. Every aspect of labor had ceased.

I might have known! The carpenters were gone, scaffolding hung idle, boards and canvas left where they lay. Work had come to a complete halt. Thomas? Thomas, of course. He would have blocked it any way he could. A wandering specter was too much for normal, rational-thinking workmen; they had simply dropped what they were doing, and fled. How would Madame take this? But undoubtedly she already knew.

All was silence as I let myself through the broad double doors and came out into the huge room which I remembered as the Grand Ballroom.

Off the first passageway beyond the ballroom were numerous closed doors and some larger empty suites whose doors stood open to reveal sheeted furniture like ghosts awaiting a séance. I glanced into a small music room, no more than a miniature replica of the vast ivory and gold salon downstairs. This lesser version contained an ancient grand piano, chairs and ottomans, and at one side, a library of what appeared to be musical references. This area too was empty of activity, like all the others. Where were the denizens of this great house? The rooms were echoing, silent.

Still farther beyond was a series of small rooms opening off a hallway and I halted before one of these, then, unable to resist, stepped inside. The apartment had once been a nursery, or at least a sleeping room, an old-fashioned wooden trundle bed pressed close to a larger cot as if for comfort. Into the headboard of the cradle was carved ''The Son of Lionel.'' There was a single window, starkly uncurtained, and beside it a wardrobe and a large chest, also very old. Intrigued, I knelt beside the chest and lifted the lid; the scent of antiquity met my nostrils.

Inside were ancient garments, creased and rusty with age; a ball gown of satin—no, it was a wedding dress! A uniform—who could this be for? Tiny shoes, a woman's shoes, and a nosegay of lavender, which had long since lost its scent, but was still bright and crisp.

I sat back on my heels thoughtfully. I could lose myself in here yet perhaps I shouldn't pry; these things were not mine. But a sense of unreality was upon me, and without my volition I was taken back into the past, away from the Château.

The ballroom—I was in the ballroom. It was a masque—no, a *grande soirée*, a *fête* celebrating my coming nuptials. The man beside me was tall; he was heavy, and he had his hand on my arm. A proprietary touch. I felt it there, a little hot, a little damp because he had drunk too freely. He always did. That, and the horses? What about the horses? He had won that day, and he was tremendously elated. He was shouting to everyone to come toast his bride-to-be. My shoulders were bare; I was in pale blue satin with sapphires, as befitted my station.

There was no other man like him upon this whole

earth—he had taken liberties, too—I blushed to think; but he was almost my husband. And I his wife? Two days hence I would truly be so.

Then the scene shifted; it was my wedding day and all were gathered in the Great Hall for the occasion. His Eminence the Cardinal—come from Calais along with a cask of his favorite wine—was ready to read the words.

I closed my eyes, almost swooning, and felt his arm around me. Then the ceremony was finished and I was his tried and true bride. I was now the Mistress of this great house, though still but a girl, barely fifteen years old! Ah, but it was a good marriage; my father, come as ambassador from the Court of the much-wived Henry to be at his daughter's wedding, was beaming and happy. I could hear the rustle of the women's lovely gowns and the murmurs of the gentlemen as they crowded forward with well-wishings; and a part of me stood aside and watched proudly.

But I am here upon my bed, and when will my labors cease? I can see my body as it writhes in pain, it does not seem to belong to me. How can this be? Yet so short a time ago it was my wedding day; my son now struggles to be born. And he is stubborn, my little one, like his father! Giselle bends to wipe the damp from my brow.

"Young Mistress," she weeps in anguish, "young Mistress, I pray, what shall I do for ye? I ha' called Old Polly but 'tis her legs again. They cannot move her where she will. Friends will try to carry her, at least she can tell us what to do!"

I feel the cold cloth on my head but it does not help. Nothing helps. My son fights to be born and my strength is gone. "No." I hear my voice rising. "I did not do it apurpose. Mathilda, she hates me—she hates everyone. She said I rode that day apurpose to destroy my son. But it is not so—I did want him, I did, I did!"

"Nay—nay, o'course ye did! Cease now, my poor baby, my poor lamb—" The haze, the gloom, it has grown thicker. The sun is blotted out and even the terrible pain has abated. Something is happening to my body but it is too late. Where is my husband, Nathaniel? He cannot be beside me now, he

is dead. He gave his life for a king who did not care. Nathaniel is dead, and I struggle for his son to be born.

The moon is very bright—see the tracery on the cobbles of the courtyard below? It is moonlight sifted through the trees. We love this room and we sit at this window, our favorite spot, to watch it. But the clouds cover the brightness—

I was aware of a voice come to me from far, far away. It was my own. "But I am not lost," I heard myself say wonderingly. "You see I know this place very well—" The words sank into silence. I rose from my knees; my throat and lips were dry and I wet my lips with my tongue. At the door I looked back. All the things, the wedding dress, the uniform, had been lovingly folded and replaced in proper order in the chest.

Nathaniel was Leonard's brother, so I'd been told. Who was Leonard, the Leonard far back? A Crecy ancestor but the name meant nothing. The whole episode was puzzling, it was colorful and tragic, but it had no significance, the name didn't mean a thing.

I made an effort to throw off my depression. Return by another way, I told myself; stop by the wine cellars, that ought to do it. I'd long wanted to visit them. I took what I assumed was the long way around, for the most direct route was by way of the kitchens.

It was a fascinating labyrinth but I hoped there would an indication of the proper turn to take.

At the end of one hallway was a set of stairs and I descended these to emerge in a service area where supplies were kept. This was of course the main floor, rear; below would be the basement, or cellars. And at last I found what I was looking for, a heavy wooden door bearing the sign Winery. I felt a vague sense of excitement. Should I have left a note? I wondered and smiled at my thought.

The door was unlocked and swung open to reveal a set of broad steps leading downward, the lower area dim but with a single bulb burning. I paused at the head of the stairs, feeling for a switch I knew must be there, and at the touch of a lever turned on the overhead lights. This was marvelous—

the long stone steps dissolving into the depths below, the stone walls, everything except the spiders and cobwebs. There was aisle after aisle and row upon row of neat wooden racks whose bottles lay snugly on their sides. The Cask of Amontillado? I hesitated suddenly, wondering if after all I should have come, but the brightness of the spacious room dispelled my nervousness. Here was no water dripping, no scurrying rats, no dank walls. Not in Madame Crecy's cellars. Everything was well kept, as well as the whole vast house.

I walked on to the end of one aisle, noting high up on the back wall several large metal boxes which obviously housed equipment. At the moment it was available, Madame's modernizing of Crecy had supplemented gas with the more convenient and practical electricity, which, save for hallway lights and the few gas heaters, was in use all over the Château. This would be the center of the electrical system, I thought.

I looked around, once more uneasy, and now aware of a distinct change in the atmosphere. The place which had been bright and cheery and alive was now dank and smelled of the grave. It was as though every ounce of air had been sucked away, and for a few brief tortured seconds I found myself gasping for breath. My skin crawled; I was conscious that my body had grown cold with perspiration. Even as I turned quickly to leave there was the creak of a door opening at the head of the steps and the scrape of a foot on the threshold.

The wine racks were in my way; I couldn't see. I stepped around them and saw the shadow of a woman poised above. Hilda Divino! I shrank back, leaning against the racks, my heart thudding against my ribs. Meeting the enemy face to face out in the open was one thing, this was something else. Why had I come down into the cellars anyway? Had the woman followed me here? Too late I recalled the warning: *Be careful of those stairs.* And I'd paid no heed, thought it meant nothing. There was one way out and Divino was blocking it.

She stood looking down. I could hear her heavy breathing

and then abruptly the big overhead lights flickered and went out. But one small bulb remained. There was only that dim glow and the aura, angry red and glimmering. And the terrible odor. Had Mrs. Divino switched off the light? No, I heard the sharp snap of the lever back and forth, and a muttered exclamation.

"Miss Kirkwood—Paulette, I know you're down there. I watched you come in." The voice was pleasant, almost silky.

I stood stiff and unspeaking. Could Divino see me? I didn't think so. The light was dim for her too, but she was coming down anyway. She was feeling her way on those stone steps but she was coming down just the same. The red shimmer followed her; it had all at once grown brighter and was all around her—I could see the reflection. It was a horrifying thing; it was anger and hate and the vitriol Jason had mentioned. Jason—if only he were here! But no, Jason would have gone long ago to his appointment, then back to the office to work late tonight as he'd said. Madame would be having dinner in her rooms, and I even knew of what that dinner consisted—veal en brochette, with mushrooms. The maid who served it would simply report if asked that Mrs. Divino was off somewhere about the house.

"They don't know where you are, do they?" the purring tones went on. "You didn't bother to tell anybody—that's a bad habit and I figured it'd get you into trouble one day. Don't you wish you had told somebody? But they won't come looking for you, they won't find you for a long, long time, because nobody comes down here much."

Was the woman crazy, demented? No, only inflamed by what festered in her head. She was at the bottom of the stairs now, the aura coming steadily with her, glowing brightly against the walls and against the floor and reflecting back. Why couldn't Divino herself see it? It was so awesomely brilliant, and it *stank*. The room reeked of scorch, of brimstone, and stung my nostrils like strong gas.

I found my voice; it seemed to me from far beyond me. "What do you want?"

"For you to get out, that's what I want! You had no

business here in the first place! We were doing fine before you came along. Now you're going to have a bad accident.'' Divino laughed harshly. ''Thought you were so smart with your fine friend, him that's travelin' the world—he was just playin' you along. Said he'd come back, didn't he? And you believed it—'' The laughter was taunting. ''Should have known better—''

I gritted my teeth. She was babbling; she would say anything. Maybe I should soothe her, try to quiet her down. ''Don't worry. You don't have to worry because I'm not going to take anything away from you. I don't want anything you've got, or ever will have.''

''You would, you would,'' the woman mumbled but the direction of my voice seemed to puzzle her, for she stopped and peered around. I would have moved; I had the strong wish to do so but knew if I stirred Mrs. Divino would see me. So long as I remained absolutely motionless she could not be sure exactly where I was; the racks cast slatted shadows and it was confusing her. I had the aura to go by, and all my senses were sharpened, like an animal at bay.

Yet sooner or later I would either have to stir from the spot or be forced to defend myself, for she was systematically proceeding up one aisle and down the next. The talk was just a diversion while she hunted me down. What did she mean to do? The shadow I glimpsed told me that she held a club of some sort upraised in her hand, a chunk of wood or length of pipe, possibly a doorstop.

My thoughts raced. There was a storage room upstairs where the wines for general table use were kept. I realized now I was in the vintage cellar, which housed only the rarest and most precious wines used for special occasions. She was right—it could be days before anyone thought to look here.

I was younger, stronger; I could undoubtedly overpower or outrun her, but sooner or later someone was going to get hurt. Badly. She was past reasoning; no amount of discussion or soothing was going to do any good. And this was Madame's valued servant, the one she'd hate to lose.

If there was only some other exit! I closed my eyes, my

wits for a moment deserting me. When I opened them again I was overcome by desperation, and cast about for something with which to arm myself. There was nothing. The strong smell grew closer and more acrid, and instinctively my hand came up and gripped the neck of the wine bottle nearest me. My fingers were wet with perspiration; I transferred the bottle to my other hand and scrubbed my palm dry against my side, then retrieved my weapon.

''Where are you? Come on, show yourself—'' she called.

I gasped and set my teeth into my lower lip. Divino stepped back; she whirled, growing wilder in her plunging search. The red aura was torn and it swirled about, trying to find its place again. The woman's voice rose sharply as she shouted hoarsely in her fury. When she reached the end of the aisle I drew back my arm and flung the bottle with all my strength. At the last moment it slipped and slammed against the wall but, miraculously, did not break.

And still she came on! Sobbing between my teeth I clutched another bottle from the rack and this time threw with greater precision. I heard the dull sickening thud as the missile struck solid flesh and Divino went down. The aura hovered over the woman's body, the glow fainter, and I sank against the racks, retching. Suddenly the light overhead came on again, then dimmed, brightened once more then finally died out altogether, and the metal boxes on the wall set up a furious humming. Except for the pulsing glow of the aura it was utterly dark in the cellar.

I stumbled to the foot of the steps, then sank to the floor in black oblivion.

CHAPTER 13

Much later I had been found at the foot of the stairs, Jason said, fainted dead away and lying on the hard cement floor. At first they'd thought I might have tumbled down the steps, but that wasn't so—thank God I wasn't hurt! Mrs. Divino had evidently suffered a dizzy spell, just as the lights went out, and she'd fallen against the racks, striking her head. She'd bruised her knee and put a gash in her scalp. It was good of me to go to her aid, Jason said, lucky for the manager that I'd decided to sightsee in this particular wine cellar, or Divino would probably be lying there still.

The doctor had come and gone; I'd been given a sedative and slept through the night. All this commotion, I thought, for nothing. I was all right, I'd just fainted, that was all, yet I was expected to remain in bed.

Madame sat in the wheelchair close by, frowning. I asked a question and Madame nodded. Hilda wasn't hurt badly, she was too tough to let a little thump on the head stop her for long. She would be up in a day or two.

"I'm awfully sorry," I said, but knew it was actually guilt I felt.

"Yes, it was too bad, but fortunate, though. It could have been worse."

The story Divino told was simple and accurate, to a point. She'd gone down to check the fuse boxes, noted two wine bottles slightly out of place, reached to adjust them and had fallen against the racks.

"She's physically sound—the doctor gave her a clean bill of health. There was no reason for her to collapse like that," the old lady observed. "Hilda's never been dizzy in her life, or sick a day she's been here. Now I want to know what really happened."

I hesitated. What could I say? My aim was poor and I put out the lights? My second try was better but could have killed the woman? Or, Divino was attacking me and I hit her with a wine bottle? The second bottle, that is, since my first knocked out the lights. Hardly! I could tell only part of the truth, and no more. Therefore I explained, carefully, that I'd seen Hilda Divino lying on the floor, her head bloodied, then the lights went out and I had fallen. I'd made it to the foot of the steps to summon help, then knew no more.

"I suppose it was the blood that caused you to faint," Madame said. "The cut on Hilda's head bled profusely, so there was a lot of it. The doorstop was at the bottom of the stairs. Two wine bottles were found out of the rack, one over by the wall where it must have rolled, the other near Hilda, where she'd dropped it. Both of them were unbroken." The old lady was still regarding me thoughtfully. "I've never known the lights to fail, not like that. I don't know what to make of it. They frightened the wits out of the servants, going on and off that way. It brought help on the run like nothing else could. Did you turn on the overhead light when you came in?"

"I turned it on," I agreed, and wished for some diversion to get the old lady's mind off the subject. If she continued in this vein, she'd soon be asking questions I couldn't answer. "I found the switch by the door right away. There was only one little bulb burning at that time. It made a wonderful difference—the cellar wasn't at all like I thought it would be."

"Then the lights went out, then on again, and you were able to see Mrs. Divino." *Not in that sequence,* I said to myself. "Did they flicker before they went off the first time?"

"Yes, once," I said honestly, glad I could tell the truth about this much at least. And it broke the spell; Madame smiled and released my hand with a little pat.

"That's it, then. I wondered. It seemed strange, though, particularly the way they dimmed and brightened, as if from interference. But I'm thankful nothing worse happened! You could have fallen down those stairs and been injured severely. Well. You need rest and here I sit, talking."

"I wish you wouldn't baby me like this," I said in acute embarrassment. "I'm all right, really. There's no earthly reason why I couldn't get up right now."

"No—no, you can't! Doctor's orders, and mine. Now just lie quietly—you can get up this afternoon. I'm going now but I'll look in on you later. And don't worry about Hilda—she's fine. If you want anything, ring. The pull is there by the bed." She smiled again. "Maybe I like babying you," she said and went out.

Jason came and went too, and now a great armful of red roses filled a vase on the table. If only they could have been from Albert! My inquiry about mail was again met with negation; a maid had brought it up and there was nothing for me.

I turned my head and closed my eyes but my thoughts whirled, endeavoring to put the pieces together.

It was Divino, of course. Always Divino. The more I thought about the tipped heater in my sitting room, the more convinced I'd become it was no accident. The water in the glass was of more sinister intent; could drinking the liquid have been fatal, or was it meant only to make me ill? The fire in my closet was a clumsy attempt to destroy my clothing and frighten me. All directed toward forcing my departure from Crecy. And her taunting remarks about Albert? She would have been aware that he had visited me, although she knew nothing of him personally. But that didn't matter; the taunts, unspeakably cruel, were calculated to cut and to demean.

The doll was something even worse, and I still cringed to think of the wanton destruction wreaked upon that lovely object. How Divino had obtained the keys I didn't know; I thought only the old lady would have had them. Yet since she possessed keys to the other rooms, might not the manager also have, or be able to get, those to the case and room as well? This was Divino's most destructive and costly attack thus far, and she had attempted to blame it on me by accusing me of having been seen with the doll in my hands earlier. Her scheme aborted, she'd waited for her chance and cornered me in the cellar.

That afternoon Jason came again and I was allowed to get up. I felt fine and had no aftereffects at all from my experience. Divino, however, was another matter. If it hadn't been for the great bitterness I knew still existed between us, I would have visited her, for despite her devilish temper and scheming I could feel sorry for the woman. Divino lay in bed in the servants' quarters, groggy from a blow on the head, her head swathed in bandages. What next, I thought, now that this most recent attempt had also failed? So long as she knew I wouldn't tell Madame, she was safe; the fight would not be called off.

Did I belong here? In spite of my brave words I knew it would be better if I left Crecy. Conditions in the household were steadily worsening, complaints were constantly being laid before the Mistress of Crecy. And the old lady was showing the strain. Could I let this go on? So long as I remained it would be no better.

Madame refused to allow me back to work for at least two days, so I gave in to Jason's urging that he be allowed to take me out into the fresh air for a while. I'd deliberated for some time about this but he'd been a perfect gentleman of late, so what harm could it do? And it was nice to be wanted! Loneliness disrupted even my night hours; I'd dreamed upon so many occasions about Albert, what he would say and do when he came back, how he would look. Most of all I never forgot his gentle caress; I'd lived it over a thousand times in my mind, thrilled to it. And waited. I was still waiting, but it seemed such a long time!

Jason was elated at my acceptance. "It's going to be a fine afternoon," he said as he helped me downstairs.

"Another slack period at the office?" I asked. "Or do you just take off any time you like?"

He shrugged airily. "There is nothing important on the docket until tomorrow morning. I am happy to say that a project I embarked upon some time ago is coming along fine, the venture a rather large one that will net considerable profit."

It was unusual for him to discuss office affairs; he'd never mentioned his dead wife and the baby either, which was strange. The grief must be so great and the hurt still so deep that he couldn't bear to talk about the accident.

"Tomorrow morning?" I repeated lightly. "You are not in trouble, I hope?" Jason opened the door for me, and I paused to take a deep breath of the fresh air.

"Why do you say that?" He looked at me quickly, then shook his head, almost at once regaining his aplomb. "Oh no, nothing of the kind. On the contrary," he said as he helped me into the buggy and spread a robe over my lap, "business is flourishing. But enough of shop talk. All ready?"

He had a small but well-kept conveyance and a fine trotter. He had, he said, considered the purchase of an automobile, they were becoming popular these days, and perhaps very soon he would do so. I pulled my short cape, the wrap Jason had insisted I bring along with me, around my shoulders, and tied the ribbons; my hat was well anchored with serviceable hatpins.

We passed through long pleasant avenues bordered by stately trees, and from there drove into a section of dwellings surrounded by grass and fences, and at last reached a scattering of small business on the city outskirts. The ride, with the wind in my face, was most exhilarating, though I felt it best to temper my enthusiasm lest it be misconstrued.

"Where are we going?" I inquired as we slowed.

He looked over, smiling. "It could be teatime, if you're interested. Remember where first we met, in that small bakery? There were only a few chairs, and if you turned around, you met yourself? Well, I know a little French café, just as small, that I'm sure you will like—they have all kinds of exotic blends of tea, as well as the plain garden variety, which is my choice. The coffee is good, too. What do you say?''

It was very tiny, a café tucked away between a cleaning establishment and a haberdasher's, but which, Jason said, had the most authentic atmosphere this side of Paris. The proprietor spoke no English, the menus were in French, the *garçons* spoke only French—and the prices, Jason mentioned with a grin, were fortunately still provincial.

"But there is a fairly wide selection and the food is excellent," Jason observed. "You'll have something besides tea or coffee, won't you?"

I had been studying the menu. I shook my head in bewilderment. "My French doesn't cover this," I admitted. "I think you had better order. A small fruit pastry for me, and tea, it doesn't matter what kind."

It was a leisurely time; for a little while my mind was washed free of anxiety, and I relaxed. Jason was affable, speaking casually of the Château, the surroundings, and his offices, which he would like to have me visit.

Afterward we toured the city and Jason pointed out things of interest. Lights began to spring up until there were a thousand of them like jewels strung around the shoulders of the city. We had driven up a hill and stopped briefly to rest the horse. Some early night bird swooped and then another, carving paths across a sunset sky. Jason swung the buggy and we moved back into the avenue.

"Have you been up in the gallery lately?" he asked. "The big one?"

I turned, surprised. "No, why?"

"*Maman* is still fighting those pictures, one of them in particular. An ancestor of Crecy's. A woman."

"I knew it wasn't Thomas's," I said. "I went through there once and his was hanging properly, but another one was missing. I just noticed a blank spot on the wall. You don't mean she's had difficulty with it, too?"

"Aside from getting the thing back from being restored, no. That one of course you haven't seen."

"Tell me about her."

"*Maman?* She married once, her husband died, she never remarried. There were no children, but you know that already. There was nobody left, so there it rested. Until you came along."

I frowned, hardly knowing what to make of the statement or his abrupt change of subject. "Until I came?"

"Well, she's looked upon me as a son but you've become the one closest to her."

"I think you must be mistaken," I said faintly.

"No, it's true. She's changed since you came. She never showed her emotions before, but she does now, I notice."

I said nothing further; we turned onto our street and pulled quietly to the curb. "And we woke no one," Jason observed. "Take a look at that old building—black as pitch. Crecy falls asleep with its chin in its soup." He gestured and asked idly, "How would you like to own that great pile?"

"Me?" I cried, shocked. "It would scare me half to death! Whatever made you say—"

But his arms had suddenly closed about me, drawing me roughly to him, his heavy mouth seeking mine. I turned my head aside at once and pulled free. "I love you, Paulette," he muttered, "I've loved you since I first saw you. Marry me!"

"No," I replied sharply, "not possibly! You don't understand!"

"I know you act as if you don't want me near you. Why? Are you worried? About something at the house?"

"That, too." The same old feeling of futility flared up. But why not tell him? Part of it at least. "Don't you have any idea what's been going on? The paranormal. Psychic activity. It has to do with Hilda Divino, her hatred."

"Are you serious?" Jason grunted his scorn. "We don't believe in witches anymore, or burn them, either. This isn't Salem—"

"Maybe not," I retorted, "but can't you see all this turmoil is affecting Madame? She can't take it."

"That's what I've been saying all along—that *Maman* should get rid of her. Now maybe you can see I'm right."

"No. Divino wants *me* out of the Château."

"Why?" he asked again.

"Who knows? Something stuck in her head."

"Don't pay any attention to Divino. She'll go, mark my words."

"She won't go. Why should she? She's a fixture at Crecy." *And I'm not,* I almost said.

"No need to be upset by something so inconsequential. Paulette—"

"No, I told you before, no!" When I pulled away again he turned ugly.

"It's that other fellow, isn't it? I saw you fawning over him. You ought to know by now he's not coming back."

The courtesy, the graciousness, were gone. I should have known better than to come! This man was strong, he could— Frightened, all I wanted was to get away and into the house where I'd feel safe. But even as my hand fumbled for the door I was struck stiff with amazement, for the Château wasn't dark anymore. Every light in the place was suddenly ablaze, every visible room vibrated with brilliance. The Château glowed like a Christmas tree; lawns, shrubbery, all the surrounding area, even the walks and the quiet street reflected those myriads of glistening lights.

"What the hell—!" Jason leaped from the buggy. I scrambled after him, my eyes fixed unbelievingly on those glaring windows, light pouring from every window Crecy owned. Even as we raced for the house excited voices broke out inside; anxious shouts and an elderly tenant's high-pitched, frightened scream.

CHAPTER 14

It was a power outage in reverse, they said, and it was the talk of the household, how the lights had so suddenly flared up, how this guest and that one had reacted to such behavior, in what situation each found himself when the event occurred.

Some of the tenants, eager to establish any possible excuse for the phenomenon, insisted it was faulty wiring, others believed that someone, a prankster perhaps, must have surely tampered with the switch boxes. For them, one or the other explanation had to suffice; I withheld judgment, but my thoughts went sniffing about. Madame, in her characteristic way, demanded immediate action.

"I'll have that wiring gone over thoroughly," she grumbled privately to me after the hubbub had begun to subside, and the house began to settle back on its haunches, the guests having at last filed back to their beds. "It seems to me if it was done properly in the first place, such a thing couldn't have happened. Electricity is nothing to tamper with! And what if it had caused a fire? I shudder to think! It won't happen again, you may be sure of that, not if I have to have every foot of cable torn out and replaced with new, from the ground up. I refuse to gamble with our guests' safety—and peace of mind—and the safety of our home." She had lately taken to referring to Château Crecy as *our* home. "I want that made clear when you contact the electric company; don't mince words. I want it checked and I want it done *now*. Insist that whatever might have gone wrong this time must not do so again.'' Madame Crecy shook her head. ''Amazing! How can every light in the Château go on at once, and apparently of their own accord? If I were superstitious, I swear—''

I wrote the note to the electric company that night and dropped it in the outgoing basket. But no one had to tell me that a plea to an electric company was futile; the trouble wouldn't be found in the wires. Lights were burning properly again and had done so since the brief lapse. Was this just another in a series of incidents which would never have taken place if I hadn't been here?

It wasn't Divino, not this time: Physically, she couldn't have managed it anyway, and she wouldn't be out of bed until tomorrow. Besides, the manager had no motive. Was it the same mischief that caused pots to jump off the hooks, a picture in a gallery to migrate?

Jason made light of the matter, of course. At breakfast the next morning he said to me, ''You couldn't have done anything to shake this creaking little group up more—''

''*I* couldn't—?''

''Figuratively speaking. Paulette, what's wrong? You seem so edgy.'' He'd apologized profusely for his boorish attitude and behaved now in the same gentlemanly way as before. ''It wasn't your fault; it wasn't anyone's fault. We simply came back in time to see it, that's all. The difficulty will be found, fixed, and forgotten.''

''Let's hope so,'' I said, but my thoughts were elsewhere. I'd stood before my window again last night staring out at the dark skyline and thinking of Albert. Remembering him, desperately trying to bring back the feel and essence of him; as time went on this seemed harder and harder to do, and tears were my only release. Had I been too forward, too eager? In my low moments I even wondered if, upon more sober reflection, he'd decided he couldn't cope with my affliction after all. But he wouldn't shrink away, would he? Not a second time!

Jason's hand on mine recalled me to the present.

"Paulette, I know how conscientious you are, but really, this is nothing. Or are you still blaming me for the other night?" he said as I drew my hand away. "It's just that I love you and want to marry you—I want you for my wife— No, don't shut me out."

I looked at the square, flushed face, so close, and felt no response. It wasn't the other night, it wasn't anything, only myself. But I didn't want to hurt him, either.

"I'm sorry for what I said, I told you that. Do I have to say it all over again? It was the jealousy of a man lashing out blindly—"

"No." I summoned a light smile. "You don't have to say anything. As a matter of fact too much has been said already—I'm due for work."

"And I'll go with you." Quickly he recovered himself, stood at my elbow, and stayed close at my side all the way up the stairs. He made only one brief rejoinder. "It's something in your past, isn't it?" To which I gave only a noncommittal reply.

For the next several days men roamed over the house from top to bottom, and, much to Madame's disgust, were too indecisive with their diagnosis.

"You'd think," Jason said at last, "for what it's costing her they'd be more forthcoming. That could help avoid such experiences in the future."

It isn't every day a sane and respectable company is called upon to ferret out trouble that isn't there, I thought, and that night actually made an attempt to summon Yvonne. It failed, of course. How could you call up a ghost when that ghost refused to appear? Yvonne was apparently keeping her distance; I hadn't seen her for weeks. No chill winds blowing through the room and stirring the curtains, no light ripple of delightful teasing laughter. No Yvonne.

Where I go my manifestations are sure to follow, I told myself bitterly, like Mary and her Little Lamb. But I had to talk to her, I had to let Yvonne, my ancestor, know where I stood before she emptied Château Crecy, before she impoverished Madame.

The furor over the lights refused to die down. Jason came

into the office one afternoon and the discussion broke out anew.

"It was bizarre," he was saying. "One minute there was a dark house and the next, blam! light was everywhere. I hope they get to the root of the trouble soon."

"They'd better," said Madame grimly. "I can't have this. It's demoralizing. You should have heard Mrs. Latour! She's hard of hearing, uses an ear trumpet, but there is nothing wrong with her voice, believe me. She was in a panic—thought we'd had an earthquake and wouldn't get down from the third floor. Mr. Utterson, he's the retired Civil gentleman on two, slept through it all. He's deaf as a post but won't admit it; this has really shaken him up. And it's not funny, not to them or to me. I maintain a proper house here, or try to, and frightening people from their beds is not my idea of proper conduct for a genteel establishment. If it ever happens again so help us I'll know it's not a simple matter of wires but somebody deliberately tampering. Or some*thing*."

"Some*thing*? What thing?" Jason guffawed. He was perched on a corner of the desk, one foot swinging, popping grapes from a bowl on his lap into his mouth one by one. He looked over at me but I maintained a stony silence; I wished I could get away but there were two more letters to finish. The talk made me nervous. Madame was skirting all around the subject I most wished to avoid and I knew that she was wondering. How long would her keen mind let it rest? She'd seen things happen that had never happened before, and there was no explanation. I hurried to complete my letters, made a stupid mistake and, with a muttered "Damn!" under my breath, corrected the error.

"Of course," Jason said. He eyed me, then Madame. "Next thing you'll be tipping tables, or maybe they'll jump by themselves. Armor tumbling downstairs, ghosts that walk and clank. Good God and double indemnity! Don't tell me you've started believing in spooks, *Maman*. It's not like you. Or do we have an invisible visitor I don't know about? Maybe a gaggle of 'em."

"Jason," the old lady said strongly, "stop babbling.

What do you know about it? You can laugh all you want but there's something funny going on—"

"Funny," agreed Jason, "that you could let such a thing cross your mind. The most matter-of-fact, down-to-earth— Why, you've managed the Château in the most logical fashion all these years—are you going to get frazzled now? I don't believe it!"

I could believe it, and Jason would never know how close he was to the truth. That night Yvonne came to me, in the middle of the night. I woke, and there she was. I lay a minute, getting my bearings. Yvonne had on a red dress, at least it looked red.

"You did wish to see me? I am sorry I did not come before—"

"Well, you're here now," I stated grimly and swung my feet over the edge of the bed and sat up. "It was you, wasn't it?"

Yvonne shrugged, but the gracefulness of the motion was lost on me. Suddenly she giggled. "It was fun, eh? Everyone running about, falling over one another. You do not think it amusing?"

"I certainly do not," I grated, thoroughly out of patience. "What do you mean by such a trick, frightening people— *old* people—out of their senses that way? What excuse do you imagine Madame Crecy can give them? If you—"

"It will come out all right," Yvonne cheerfully broke in. "One thing, as you say, leads to another. You do not believe that? I know. A little spice, a little laughter to do good. And it will be all right. You did nothing so I had to."

"You're talking in riddles!" I snapped. "*I* didn't do anything? What was I supposed to do?"

Yvonne sighed, shrugged again, and became evasive. "You do not like me anymore," she said plaintively. "You will not be seeing me much longer anyway. Cannot things be pleasant for the time left? Thomas says I should have done something much worse—to wake you up, to wake up this house. But you do not understand. You see, events must proceed. Since they did not, I had to intervene. Sometimes," she added, "it is necessary."

I shook my head in exasperation. "No, I don't understand. I'm not angry with you—at least I don't dislike you,
how could I? But if you would give me one good reason for
what you did maybe I could accept it. And what do you
mean, you won't be around much longer?" But I was
talking to the wall; Yvonne had smiled, shrugged again, in
typically French fashion, and faded.

Yvonne had said nothing about my battle with Divino nor
given me an opportunity to do so. Did she consider that also
of no importance, the mounting tension at Crecy of no
consequence? And there was no plausible reason, so far as
I could see at any rate, for "shaking up the house" as she
termed it. The situation was unsatisfactory and I was even
more puzzled than before.

The tenants knew nothing of the difficulties in the
kitchens, nor did the manager appear to them, when they did
see her, as other than her usual dour self. But Katrine left,
soon to be followed by Francie; Madame grimly wrote out
their references along with the checks for the customary two
weeks' severance pay. Crecy's employ was much sought
after and as a result the two posts were filled almost at once
from a long waiting list.

Nor was the matter of the doll at an end. Madame told me
that Hilda continued to agitate about it.

"She was absolutely convinced you meant to get her into
trouble. I'm sick of hearing about the whole thing. So far as
I am concerned the episode is finished. The rubies were
found by a girl emptying the carpet sweeper—who knows
where they were picked up? I've sent the doll out to be
repaired and it will be back shortly—after it is, I defy
anyone to mention the business again! In the meantime, I'm
going to have to forestall any more of this leaking out to the
tenants, and I think I've struck upon a solution. We'll have
the collection on display, a showing, and what amounts to a
guided tour. It will give an opportunity to air a little family
history, and they'll love it. I'd like you to pour, if you
will—we'll have tea in the Trophy Room—say a week from
Friday?"

"Me?" I said.

"Of course. I'll give you a list of what's to be done. In general, as you know, the Trophy Room is kept locked—the tenants rarely go up there anyway, and few have seen the collection. But now we'll make a fine party of it. I used to put on entertainments of one kind or another quite often, but of late I'd grown away from it—too much to do, I expect. But at this time I do feel something is required to strengthen what has always been a good, stable image. Don't you?"

"Oh, yes," I agreed. Something else should be done, too; there'd been further altercations in the kitchen and because of the manager's heavy hand another girl had quit, the third in two weeks. "There was that new girl who applied—did you hire her?"

"I hired her." The old lady said wearily, "I can't have my household ruled by cuffs and snarls. I scarcely know what to do. For years we'd gotten on well here—Hilda's temper never got out of hand. Now it seems boxed ears and sarcasm are daily fare. The girls do not like it and I don't blame them. The cooks don't like it, either; one of them threatened to quit the other day. If she doesn't mind her p's and q's, Hilda will go! Perhaps our party will do everybody good." Madame was showing mental strain herself, in the deepened lines of her face, the dark circles under her eyes that attested to sleepless nights, and in the sharper, more frequent episodes of impatience.

I left the office to pursue my errands and ran into Jason. He suggested dinner out at a nice restaurant but I refused. Madame had been quite upset, I said, and under no condition would I leave her.

"It's been hot today, sultry," I added. "She's been talking about going down into the garden. She'd love to have late tea by the pool, but it will probably have to wait for another time. It seems to be clouding up."

"And I'll be doing what I should be doing," Jason said ruefully. "A case is coming up shortly. Well, if I can't make any headway here, I'll be off."

A monotonous splat-splat of rain that would eventually drench the earth began, and Madame Crecy sent word that she would take a postponement of our outing in the garden since she had an aversion to wet feet. She would be in her office working on the lists until bedtime, why didn't I look in later?

I smiled at that. There had been similar occasions when the old lady merely wanted company. I bathed and dressed quickly, took a brief meal in the dining room, and went up to Madame's quarters. Maybe this celebration would be good for the old lady too, give her something to think about besides unpleasantness. There had been enough of that lately.

"I thought I'd get in an hour or so of work," Madame said to me when I joined her, "while I had the chance. Tomorrow's delivery day and the place will be crowded with tradespeople. After that we'll really get busy on the festivities. Did Jason leave?" she asked, and at my nod said, "He seems to have a fairly heavy schedule right now." She pushed herself back from the desk and folded her hands in an unaccustomed restful gesture. "They had to send away for material to match the Manona doll's torn robe, and it won't be back in time for the showing. We'll go on without it—one won't be missed anyway, there are plenty of others. How is your dressmaking coming along?"

"Just fine." I'd had a fitting a few days ago and would have another soon. "One gown is particularly beautiful," I said warmly. "Quite a dress-up affair, all of floaty, gauzy material, but simple, with a lovely drape."

"The creamy orange I suggested? Not orange, really, more like orange whipped with cream. I call it orange."

"The same." I'd loved the color too and I'd liked the soft pinks and yellows as well, but as Madame said, they were not for me.

"Wear the orange at the showing," she said now.

I nodded. I got up and took a turn around the room, suddenly ill at ease. Down in the garden it was dusk; only shafts of light from these upper windows slanted through the raindrops to pierce the gloom. Where was Albert now? What was he doing? Was he all right? If there was only some way I could reach him! But between us there was that blank, impenetrable wall of silence.

"Were you going somewhere, did you have something planned?" Madame spoke behind me. "It's just occurred to me that I might be a bothersome old lady."

Her remarks broke my pensive mood. "No." I smiled, then sat down and reached for a coffee cup. After that we sat quietly for a time in the relaxed fashion of two people whose relationship had deepened to a point where speech was no longer necessary.

"I enjoy your being here with me," the old lady said at last. "I take great comfort in it. Are you looking forward to the party?"

"Oh yes. I think it will be fun. Is there anything you would like me to do for you?"

"No, nothing." Madame shook her head. "If we feel like taking it a bit easy we should do just that. I tell myself the world will turn anyway, it always has—not that I profit much from my own advice. But I've been meaning to speak to you of something and wanted to do so before the show. Would you like to ask me about any of the characters represented in the collection? If you know more about them, I think you might enjoy it better."

I took a sip of my coffee. "No," I said, "they tell their own story. And you've told me a little already. I prowled the nursery upstairs, too; you know, the little room off the long hall, where you can look down on the circular seat? I opened the chest," I confessed.

"Well enough. Nothing in there should be kept hidden. Nathaniel was the one who owned the uniform, he took after his grandfather, old Bideau Crecy, a professional soldier. Young Nathaniel loved that life. He joined when he was twelve but he was big for his age and managed to stay in. They weren't hiring babes warm from their mother's knee, even then! We've tales come down to us from that era. Thomas's son was named for him. Nathaniel married a lovely girl of good family."

Her father was ambassador to the Court of England, my mind echoed, *I know about that.*

"She became pregnant right away, or already was. At any rate Nathaniel got his call not long before the baby was to be born—he'd been home only a few months when the siege began. There were always sieges—France hoped to regain Calais from England's Henry, you see. Nathaniel was put in command of a garrison besieging that city. He never came back.''

"The girl?"

"Honorée? She died giving birth to her child."

Of course, my thoughts reiterated. *I was there.* "And the baby?"

"Is also an ancestor of that rogue upstairs—Thomas, the one you saw in the picture."

"I . . . see." More of the past fell into place; it laid a wreath on a lonely grave. "Who was Leonard?" I asked curiously.

"Nathaniel's brother. An unusual strain runs through the blood—I'll tell you about it sometime."

"I have an old brooch," I said, "an heirloom left me by my grandmother. Since I know how interested you are in such things, you might like to see it. I'll run up to my room and get it—it'll only take a minute."

It took longer than I expected; the brooch wasn't in my small jewel case where I usually kept it, but I located it at last wrapped in a handkerchief tucked into a corner of my dressing table drawer. With the brooch in my hand I descended the stairs again, and met Jason at the door.

"I couldn't keep away," he said cheerfully. "What have you got there?"

"Something Madame wanted to see."

We entered and I laid the brooch on the desk before her. The old lady bent over the trinket, then straightened abruptly. "May I keep this here? I'd like to examine it tomorrow when the light is better." Then I saw how white her face was. "Get a carpenter up here to fix that chock in the ramp. I couldn't get Hilda on the pull just now and went out to see where she was. The chock was loose and I almost lost my balance." She added grimly, "I'll die one day but not before my time and not by falling down my own steps!"

Jason came to his feet, an odd, frozen look on his face.

"It's too late to get one now," I said dumbly, still in

shock. "I'll attend to it first thing in the morning." I shook
myself. "You won't be using that ramp again tonight
anyway. If you'd thought to, don't," I said, and did not
realize how possessive and peremptory the words sounded.

"Those chocks should be checked regularly," Jason
pointed out. "I've mentioned it before, more than once. Too
much depends on them. A wheelchair could take a nasty
header from the top of the ramp—any one of them—and it's
a long way down. You'd certainly be killed. What's wrong
with the chock, could you see? It wouldn't take much, even
a loose screw—"

"The rug was cut."

Jason whirled; my gasp was audible in the room.

"Stay here," Jason told Madame, and I followed him
into the hall. There was no one in the hallway when we
reached it, and the balcony was empty as well. Jason bent
over the small lump beneath the carpet, examining it
closely.

"*Un*cut," he pointed out briefly at last and we stared at
each other in disbelief. "This hasn't been tampered with.
Can you see right there? No sign of a break, no marks,
nothing. Why do you suppose she said that?" Jason shook
his head, sat back on his heels. Again he bent to look and
again sat back. "I've never known her to make such a
statement before," he said. "She's the most level-headed
person I know."

I said nothing. I stood up, frowning. "She could have
only thought she saw a broken one," I said slowly.
"The light, you know, it's soft in here. Perhaps," I added,
"she has worried a lot about these things, and who
wouldn't? She could have pictured them loosened so many
times that this time it became a reality to her. I can't
discredit her story; she *thought* she saw it loose." I looked
again at the carpet, uncut, smooth, exactly as it should be, as
I had seen it myself countless times, the small triangular
wooden pieces fitted beneath it as solid as the Rock of
Gibraltar.

Or were they? "Wait a minute," I said excitedly. "Do
you have a knife—any kind of a knife?"

Jason had a small one. I looked at the knife. There was
something on the tip of the blade. "Go on, use it. It won't
hurt. It's just a piece of apple. I peeled an apple earlier."

Once more I knelt, then inserted the blade carefully into
the carpet just above the first chock. A slit, almost invisible,
appeared, a sticky substance oozing from it. "Glue," I
stated. "See?" I touched it with a finger. "The glue would
have dried and the break mended itself by morning and no
one the wiser." I pressed hard on the chock with the heel of
my hand; it was loose. Put the wheelchair's weight on it and
it would have slipped. "She was right."

We got slowly to our feet. "Who?" Jason asked, and I
shook my head, but inside I was sick with apprehension.

CHAPTER 15

Madame must have had her own ideas about who cut the carpet, causing her near mishap, but she refused to say, and I dared not ask for fear of upsetting her further. But the chocks were thoroughly investigated from one end of the house to the other; moreover, every day I made it my business to quietly patrol those she most frequently used.

There were confrontations in Madame's office with Divino and other servants, the results of which I never learned. During this time the old lady worked furiously and, without realizing that she did so, worked me the same way.

It was another Monday morning and already the Mistress of Crecy had been up two hours, breakfasted, and was launched into the day's affairs.

"Post these on the bulletin board," she instructed, "in the west foyer. I want the showing to be well publicized. And we'll need these printed; there's a concern in town that's filled orders for me before. You'll find the address marked there in the book. They're little leaflets the guests might like to keep. Then a half-dozen invitations—will you take them personally to these people? There's Mrs. Cromwell; she doesn't get about readily because of her bad back—she might miss the notice. She's on the second floor, room 214. Mrs. Edis, in 216, is hard of hearing—it could be necessary to rout her out, gently, of course. Mrs. Carlysle in 324 is another recluse, you may have to pry her off her bed and out of her chocolate box; she's mountainous. Mr. Weston and Mr. Brabington, in 326 and 340, I've jotted them down—'' Madame handed me a list. "That makes five. Then Mr. Owen in 390, down at the end of the hall. I've always suspected him of actively pursuing the ladies, even at eighty-plus, but I've had no complaints and that's all I can ask. Nevertheless take care, he's not been above a fatherly pinch or two with the maids and might try it with you. That's all, for the moment."

I'd written my note, so I picked up the envelopes, and rose.

"Paulette?"

I turned. The old lady smiled. "Cheer up. Nothing's happened and nothing is going to. If you go around with a long face you'll make me unhappy, too. Somebody has to keep this pot boiling, and I need help."

I shrugged and summoned an answering smile as I went out. *Sufficient unto the day,* I was thinking. *But what next*?

I went past the bulletin board and did as I had been requested, then climbed the stairs again to the second floor. Since the night of the power difficulty when Mr. Brabington had been seen in the hallway gallantly sheltering two old ladies beneath his wing, romance was suspected, but nothing so far had come of it.

When I came to Mrs. Cromwell's room, the door was properly open and the two old persons, Mrs. Cromwell and Mr. Brabington, sat cozily playing cribbage, knee to knee. Mr. Brabington got to his feet at once; Mrs. Cromwell, with her puff of white hair, swooped to shake my hand with the darting progress of a moth. Tendering my invitations, I was astonished by the response.

"Of course! Dear Miss Kirkwood—it is Miss Kirkwood, I presume? We should be happy to come, Hector and I. Won't we, Hector?" Hector managed a smile. "We have had so few celebrations in the house of late, but once in a while there's some excitement, eh? The night of the lights—that's what I call it, the night of the lights—wasn't that shocking?" She smiled fondly at her companion. "Hector says one ought to be concerned about what caused it. He was wondering—what did the report say was wrong?"

I spoke reassuringly. "Most likely it was due to the renovation—considerable work was being done in the other part of the building, you know, and occasionally wiring can become involved. But everything has been thoroughly checked and it won't happen again."

The explanation seemed to satisfy Mrs. Cromwell for she nodded briskly. "Yes. Yes, of course. Though I must admit I found it stimulating." She glanced back over her shoulder at Hector. "Madame Crecy is so thoughtful, such a grand lady. It will be delightful to have something going on again. This showing, for instance—dolls, did you say? Heirlooms? How extraordinary! We have missed our little fun times, haven't we, Hector? Hector was remarking just yesterday how we used to enjoy them. Friday at two, you say?"

The kindly Mr. Brabington murmured, "It is kind of you to let us know, Miss Kirkwood. You have been keeping busy, haven't you? We have seen you around and about, knew who you were, but so nice to meet you face to face at last. I—we—will be there, of course."

I went on down the hall with a fleeting sympathy for the outflanked Mr. Brabington, whose days of freedom were numbered. When I reported back, Madame would be amused to learn of the miraculous cure; Mrs. Cromwell's bad back obviously bothered her no longer.

Next, room 216 and Mrs. Edis. She might have been posted just inside the door, it opened so quickly at my knock. Clearly I was not the hoped-for caller, but Mrs. Edis recovered herself, and when I explained my errand, she accepted with surprise and pleasure.

"Well, you know Madame Crecy used to do this before—musical evenings, gallery tours, and the like—but she hasn't for some time now. I hope this means she is starting them up again. We enjoyed them so much. Social activity can be of great benefit no matter what the age, don't you think?" She peered wistfully over my shoulder. This was one of the two ladies rejuvenated by Mr. Brabington on that fateful night, but it was the other, Mrs. Cromwell, who apparently had the edge. A pity. I would have preferred it to have been Mrs. Edis, tall, thin, devoid of frills and feathers, but sincere.

The next stop was the Carlysle suite. That portly lady had been asleep and as a result she was slow in answering the summons. I apologized for disturbing her and explained the mission, chatted a moment, and left. Weston, in 326, took me up another floor and I delivered my envelope and departed, retaining a memory of a small pink gentleman floating in a sea of Bay Rum.

The last candidate was rotund, jolly, apple-cheeked, with a bushy gray beard, above which roved a pair of bright blue eyes, keen and too exploratory.

"Well, well, Miss Kirkwood! What is this?" He clutched at my fingers, and I extended the envelope with the explanation. "A party? I wouldn't miss it for the world—good to get out, you know, socialize." He emerged nimbly from his doorway, but I sidestepped, pleading shortness of time, and so managed my escape.

Having made my deliveries, I turned toward the dressmaker's. Mrs. Able's headquarters were on the fourth floor, front. Here the light was best and tall windows not only enhanced the large room but permitted the greatest amount of light possible. Bright rugs were on the floor, the walls adorned with colored prints of fashionable ladies in the latest *couture*. A few long tables held bolts of vari-colored cloth, others were spread with sewing paraphernalia. Dress forms of every height and shape imaginable stood in the corners. I'd been fascinated by the room when I'd first seen it, and I was fascinated now.

Mrs. Able hurried forward, smiling, the same energetic little person, radiating confidence and good cheer.

"Hello, Mrs. Able," I greeted. "Should I have come earlier?"

"No, my dear, this is fine. And we'll get right to it."

I nodded. "The dark green bombazine?"

"Will be ready next week. The creamy orange, also next week, sooner if you wish. I can put the others aside and complete that first. I think you needn't come for fittings for the other two. Would you like to try on the green one now?''

The business was finished in short order, and I took my leave. Truly, the little lady was a miracle-worker, possessed of the ability to transfer lengths of shapeless material into creations of beauty and distinction.

There were a few tea-takers in the dining room; those who knew me smiled, others nodded pleasantly. I drank my own beverage, then on impulse, let myself out the wide doors and went around the house by the front way.

The late afternoon sun was still bright and warm and the young robins, hatched out in the old maples beside the house, orchestrated a cacophony of sound. There were at least three nests of them; string dangled from one careless homemaker's abode and waved gently in the breeze. Diligent parents came in relays with beaksful of worms. It was pleasant here, I thought, so pleasant, but how long would it be home?

I turned abruptly and ascended to my quarters. Before I reached them I saw Hilda Divino moving into a doorway down the hall. I looked after the woman with the keenest desire to follow; all the worry, my frustration and pent-up anger, threatening to boil over.

But a greater suspicion held me back and I continued on to my room. Divino, the likely suspect, or was it only meant to appear that way? Jason had been vociferous in his denunciation of the manager. She was guilty, fire her at once, get her out of the house before she killed somebody. In line for a fat plum, he'd insisted, why wouldn't Divino be of a mind to hurry things along? Dead men told no tales, nor women either, and the mutilation of the carpets, if discovered, could be blamed on any of the lesser menials.

All this I had considered, but—and here my thoughts ground to a halt then moved forward again, step by step—was Jason himself above reproach? He was aware of how things were going in the house, the fact that Hilda Divino, the acknowledged heiress, was alienating herself. But wasn't Madame being pressured to see her in a bad light? Madame trusted him with her affairs, he even called her *Maman*—Mother. The charm which had so captivated

the old lady could be a blind for his true motives, in which
case I had become too much the confidante and companion
to the old Mistress of Crecy not to be a thorn in his flesh.
He'd as much as said so, in the buggy that day. *She looked
upon me as a son, but you've become the one closest to her.*
There might have been more meaning in those words than
I'd thought then.

And in the Old Wing when I had nearly fallen—could I
have been pushed? No more than a gentle nudge that I
couldn't, now, in looking back upon it, be sure hadn't
actually happened? Then the substance on the knife blade; it
wasn't apple, as Jason said. *It looked like glue!* I'd been
upstairs searching for my brooch; Madame was in her office
with the door closed. When had Jason come? How long had
he been there before I returned and we entered the office
together? I couldn't see myself as a threat, but I could
certainly be troublesome. With me out of the way, Divino
ousted, who was left?

Or from another angle: with Madame gone and Divino
inheriting, could he have the *directrice* declared mentally
incompetent and, as Crecy's legal representative, take over
himself? He must be fairly certain that the plan would work.
If he was the one who cut the chock. I had no certain
answers for these things; I only knew my position in this
house was daily growing more untenable. I had to leave
Crecy.

I sat staring at the window, seeing nothing beyond it.
Should I be bold, straightforward? *This household will settle
down if I am no longer around to complicate matters;
Divino's efforts will cease with no target. One way or
another Jason can get rid of Divino, then he'll have the field
to himself.* So this was a power struggle, a fight over money,
the institution of Crecy and all it stood for. The situation
became clear now, and it sickened me. Money. Through the
ages people had fought and died for it. Fought and *killed* for
it.

Restless, I rose and left the room. When I reached the
ramp nearest the old lady's door, I walked it slowly, testing

each chock as I descended. No trouble here; everything was solid.

Long before reaching the office I could hear voices inside, Madame's raised harshly.

"I won't have her maligned! I want no more of this talebearing. And the next servant you discharge, you go, too!" A hand sharply struck the desktop. "I am sick of this uproar!"

"You can't fire me! I'm almost family, you said so yourself! I've worked for—"

I wasn't going to get caught in this again! I moved away rapidly. The office door was yanked open, Divino emerged.

"Just a minute, you!" I stopped and turned; she strode up to me. "What have you been telling Madame?"

I faced the furious woman. "I told her nothing," I retorted. "Why? Do you have something to hide?"

The manager advanced a step; I held my ground. "I wouldn't try it," I said through clenched teeth, returning her stare, then turned on my heel and walked away. Before entering Madame's door I looked back. The aura—the stinking, red-tinged aura that always accompanied the dark woman, was hurrying to catch up.

"Don't you pay any mind," a familiar small voice said behind me. It was Yvonne. "The aura is nothing; we see them often. It will not hurt you. But beware of the other."

"Who—Mrs. Divino?"

But Yvonne was gone. Tight-lipped, I went on into the office.

"Jeanette, one of the serving maids," Madame told me, "was struck by flying glass. Hilda swears the girl threw the jug, the girl swears she did not. Again Hilda discharged the girl, though she has been strictly forbidden to take a hand in such matters. It is the last time!"

"Can't the girls come to you?" I asked.

"They could, if they dared. But Hilda has them cowed. I've never seen a person exert such influence! It's uncanny. And all right in its place—authority is a wonderful thing if not abused. The help will obey her and that is all to the good, but I will not have it this way. I will *not*!" The old lady's jaw was set, her eyes stormy. Now was no time to broach the subject of leaving, it would have to wait. Besides, there was the doll showing; I was expected to be there. What, I wondered, would these excesses of emotion do to her?

I found out, the next afternoon. It was about three o'clock and we had been working on ledgers when the old lady suddenly dropped her hands to the desk, an odd look pinching her face. "Call Jason—if you will. And that will be all—for today."

I jumped up and ran around the desk, frightened. "Do you want me to get a doctor? Is there anything I can do?"

"No! I'm all right. See if Jason—is still here." And under her breath she added, "I hope I haven't waited—too long."

I hurried from the room; a maid said Jason was downstairs. "Get him!" I snapped, then returned to Madame. I'd been dismissed but couldn't bring myself to go. "I don't want to leave you alone! Let me stay at least until he gets here."

"No, I'm all right now." And she did look better; there was color in her cheeks again and her lips had lost that gray, papery appearance. "Actually I won't need Jason after all, but since you've already called him it's all right. I've been meaning to settle something with him anyway and this is as good a time as any. I'm just overtired, that's all, and overwrought. I'll take the rest of the afternoon off, read and relax. Run along now," she said as I still hesitated, "come back and have tea with me at six. All right?"

It had to be all right. I went out, still deeply worried. I well knew Madame's tremendous energy but also knew what the old lady had been going through these past weeks. The situation couldn't continue this way; it would kill her. She was far from young and even great strength could burn out.

At six, after a very light dinner, I presented myself for tea, as Madame expected. On a small table at her elbow reposed the tea things. The desk had been cleared and she looked well and seemed in high spirits.

She had been looking at my brooch and now turned it over in her hands almost caressingly. "You have an extraordinarily fine piece here, did you know that? I doubt there could be another like it anywhere. Have you examined it closely? Very closely? Come, I'll show you." She wheeled herself rapidly over to the larger desk lamp and switched it on, and from a drawer extracted a magnifying glass. "Lean closer," she instructed, "see—there? Near the clasp? The initials of the French royal house, and the Valois cross. Your brooch came originally from Milan, probably by way of Louis—Louis XIV—as a gift to someone who had done him a particular service. There is a further inscription on it—a small triple cross. Very tiny. You will need the glass and have to look very closely to decipher it. It means the brooch was in France at the time of the Revolution. It must have meant a great deal to someone; whoever smuggled it out risked his life. Would you have any idea who that was?"

I shook my head. "None at all," I said. The value of the brooch, its antiquity, concerned me less than what I must say, and soon, to Madame for Madame's own sake. I could not bring myself to burst that bubble now, to bring shock to those warm old eyes. Later. It would have to be later, and at just the right time.

CHAPTER 16

The weather had turned spitting and cold, a raw wind blew and rattled the maples outside the windows. The small robins were miserably silent and I imagined them huddled in their sodden nests, the parents endlessly bringing those worms. The loose string tossed wildly; the leaden skies of summer bore the look and feel of fall.

Jason came that evening; I was having dinner in the dining room, and he sat down beside me. "It isn't often I catch you like this."

"Catch" was the right word, I thought wearily, and in an effort to change the subject, asked, "A busy day?"

"Yes. And you?"

"Also. Great preparations are under way for the party."

He turned suddenly. "I'd make you a good husband, Paulette, marry me!" His tone had altered; his fingers lingered on my arm but I pulled away. When he spoke again his words were edged with anger and there was a strange finality in his speech. "All right, then! I've made myself clear, I can't do any more." He said abruptly, "Day after tomorrow is *Maman*'s birthday."

"What?" My hand flew to my mouth. "I didn't know! Nobody told me," I said. "She'll be eighty-three?"

"That's right. The servants and tenants get together for some wholehearted well-wishing. It's a ritual—a tradition. Sunny Wednesday was built around the birthday."

"Sunny Wednesday?"

"The same. That is what it was first called, and still is—Wednesday, Thursday, Friday, whatever. And it can rain before or after but better be nice on The Day or heaven will hear of it. I think the household gets together and burns heathen incense or something."

I thought back. Someone in my family had done that too—a grandmother, a great-aunt?—and it was done for me, when I was very small, a silly little play-game abandoned when I grew older. Only it seemed strange now—the similarity of the two.

"Birthday cakes and everything?"

"No birthday cake. The shoe is on the other foot. *Maman* descends to dinner in the dining room, and all the well-wishers line up while she shakes hands and bestows gifts—you know, as in olden times, distributing the largesse of the Manor."

I looked away. It was charming and sweet, just the sort of tradition the grand old lady would follow. I could imagine what havoc my announcement, coming on the eve of this celebration, would create, and I resolved I would wait until after birthday and display were over and I could talk to Madame in private, quietly and logically, with no interruptions. I would explain then that I felt it best to leave, and give as much of the reason for it as I could.

The day of Madame's birthday did dawn clear and bright. The earth was damp but warm, ground fog rose but quickly dissipated under the brilliance of sunshine and blue sky. The robins began the work of the day and old Noonan, the gardener, came to ask Madame if she wished the yellow roses for the celebration and should he pick them now. He doffed his cap, the smile reaching to his rheumy old eyes.

"Happy birthday, Ma'am, an' many more o' 'em. I wished for that last year, I can recollect."

"That you did, Noonan, and the one before, and before that! Thank you. No, we'll save the roses for the latter part of the week—they'll last that long, won't they? Then we'll decorate the Trophy Room with them. Some may still be good for the wedding. Did you know we are going to have a wedding, Noonan? Mrs. Cromwell and Mr. Brabington, in 204 and 310.''

The old man said stubbornly, ''Nothing's as important as your birthday, ma'am, if I may say so.''

''That's nice of you, but no.'' Madame smiled. ''Dinner in the dining room will be the same as usual, no decorations. You may have the roses ready for Friday afternoon—better pick them in the morning and see they're kept cool and in a dark place so they won't open so much—have someone let me know when they're ready.''

''Aye. An' thank you, ma'am.''

I closed the door after him, turned to Madame and said, ''He worships you. You inspire awe in the people here.''

''Noonan's a good man,'' she said, ''a good gardener.''

There was no work as such on this day. Early I had gone out by hired buggy, bringing back with me a little box which I carried to my quarters and wrapped, attaching a card—all in haste, but I could not do otherwise. The old lady called me shortly afterward, to explain the procedure.

''There is a bit of ritual about my birthday,'' she said and indicated cartons filled with gifts sitting upon the floor. Each gift was of a different shape and size. I thought she must have been up all night at the chore, but she appeared rested and happy. Apparently she had put all unpleasantness aside for the celebration.

''I want you to stay and help. I need you.''

''Yes,'' I managed. And if my joy in the occasion was tempered with the sadness of the knowledge of my imminent departure, no one knew of it but myself. We made our way to the dining room, and I watched as, one by one, Madame's guests came up to greet her, each in his or her own way, and each receiving his tissue-wrapped package. A tie clasp here, a bracelet, a scarf or necklace there, a knitted shawl, a book—there was an endless variety of objects, each obviously chosen with great care. And they loved her well. All this I saw, standing by her side, reading it in the manner in which they spoke to her, the sincerity of their congratulations.

"You see, Mistress, the sun did shine," little Janette said shyly, and prepared to bear away a box of crumpled tissue and ribbon.

"Ah, that it did." Madame beamed.

"Happy birthday, Mistress."

"Thank you, Janette. Mrs. Edis, you look well—" Though in truth the woman did not. It must have taken the strongest kind of courage to come here at all. Presently Jason entered, placing a small box on the table beside Madame, then a second one.

"It was finished," he said briefly, "so I picked it up. Happy birthday, *Maman*." He bent to bestow a kiss on her cheek.

"In the lap of the gods," Madame replied. "Another year and another mile. At my age, a miracle. Jason, you shouldn't have. You're breaking a precedent, an established rule, and why did you do it?"

"I might feel worse if I didn't," Jason said and moved around beside me. His glance was unreadable, but there seemed to be something waiting in it.

The meal was served. Someone stood up to make a speech and, childlike, we sang a birthday melody. Madame inclined her head, listening gravely until it was finished. Then she looked up.

"Thank you all," she said clearly and her voice carried to the far corners of the room. "My gratitude for your good wishes. And now I have an announcement to make."

She told them about the wedding and the bride- and groom-to-be stood up, acknowledging the excited squeals, the thunderous applause, then resumed their seats.

"Bloody bore," Jason observed. "I could have done without this."

Madame had heard; she glowered over her shoulder. "You could show some respect."

Jason said nothing. We returned Madame to her suite, and she insisted that we stay for a while. Jason had given her a gold pin with the family crest and her initials on it. The other box contained my brooch. The clasp had been loose and Madame had sent it out to be repaired. I had little to offer; on that hurried trip I'd purchased a small jewel case of red enamel banded with gold, and lined with red velvet. It was not costly or even strictly beautiful but the best I could manage upon such short notice. I thought the gift woefully inadequate for someone who had so much.

But the old lady loved it. The box now reposed on the bookcase across the room, gleaming palely in the light.

"As you know, I give gifts on my birthday," Madame said. "Jason, you already have mine—" Jason lifted his hand, a beryl ring adorned his little finger. "Paulette, there is a reason yours cannot be given yet. There is only one request I have to make, that you do not protest my present to you. You are to accept, because that is my wish."

I could only nod my agreement, and puzzled over what the token might be. We left shortly after; I felt the old lady needed rest.

I walked downstairs to the front door, and stood on the porch in the early twilight. Again, Jason had followed. There seemed little to say.

"It's odd, isn't it," I said at last, "how one changes? I remember when I was so afraid of her I was tongue-tied. Now our positions seem reversed; I want to watch over her, protect her in everything she does."

"Do you have any idea what she's giving you?"

"No, I don't. I'm not a child any longer, it doesn't matter. I'd much rather she didn't give me anything at all. Why should she?"

Jason shrugged. "Her idea." I said nothing. "Anything wrong?"

"Tired."

Abruptly he nodded. "Good night," he said and strode down the walk. If only I could see Albert come up that same walk! My eyes blurred with tears.

I climbed the stairs to my room, there to sit quietly staring out into the milky moonlight shining over the silent garden. All was bathed in that pearly opalescence, even the garden with its shrubs and potted plants seemed to shimmer as if viewed through water, indistinct, like a dream. It was clouding again. Had the Power which held the house in sway paused only long enough to honor the Mistress of Crecy on her birthday? The night crept in with its dampness and chill and I drew a sweater about my shoulders, still looking out into that cobwebby moonlight and hearing in the silence the creak of the old house as it settled.

Night, someone once said, was to the Château a surrender, a relinquishing of the affairs of the day with a long happy sigh. But from what I had seen, it was more a time for putting in curlpapers, applying wrinkle cream, and groaning in relief while pushing creaky toes between smooth cool sheets. Either way it was a sigh of contentment, a comfortable lights-out-and-don't-disturb relaxation.

Disrobing, I realized how long it had been, other than a brief word from Yvonne, since I'd had a visitation. Wouldn't it be ironic if now, almost on the eve of my departure, they had decided not to come again, and I might be normal? The room was still; it was pleasant and gracious and peaceful, but wrapped in a cocoon of loneliness, I cried myself to sleep.

The next day was a busy one and I worked steadily until noon. There was lunch, after which Madame sent me to find a maid with a message for Divino. The old lady wanted the yellow vases—the yellow only—for the Trophy Room. They were to be set up and everything arranged, then she herself would make an inspection.

I went out, leaving Madame remarking acidly upon the quality of coffee these days. They'd change blends. Couldn't expect people to—

The maids were obviously busy elsewhere for I encountered not a one—this wing of the house was being decorated from top to bottom—and I stumbled upon Marie quite by accident. The girl was on her knees sweeping up the remnants of lunch from an overturned tea cart and she looked up tearfully.

"What happened?" I demanded.

"Oh, Mademoiselle, I do not know! That Divino again—I think she do these things on purpose to get us into trouble. She say the door slam in her face. I do not believe it—how could I do it? I was here—!'' She turned her cheek, and I saw an angry red weal across it. Divino had slapped her, hard. Marie was in no state to brave the manager.

''I'm sorry,'' I said grimly. ''Where is Mrs. Divino now?''

''In the china closet—the one at the end of the hall.'' Marie hiccuped, and began crying again as she bent to her task. There was nothing to do but go myself.

The door was closed and it stuck and I had to tug to get it open. Then I stared, aghast. Mrs. Divino stood in a welter of broken crockery, she had a set of bowls in her arms and was reaching for a platter above her head.

Seeing the woman in trouble I spoke involuntarily. ''Here, let me help—''

The manager greeted me with even less than her usual civility. ''You witch! You bitch! Why don't you get out of here and leave me alone? I don't need any help!'' Her face was livid, the stench of the aura overpowering. The storage closet was a shambles; there was scarcely an unbroken piece of china remaining. One of the shelves hung by its end, and all the stacked crockery had slid from it to a littered heap upon the floor.

''Did you do this?''

''No!''

''Was it this way when you got here? Nothing's ever happened as bad as this, has it?''

Divino glared; I almost thought she meant to hurl the platter, but the dish slipped from her fingers. ''You ought to know,'' she yelled. ''You're trying to drive me away, honeying up to the old lady, making her do your will, and now this!'' She spoke in a curious singsong. ''I heard about evil spirits and now I seen 'em. You're conjurin' 'em up, you're in league with the Devil. They want to—''

''Stop it!'' I broke in. ''Stop it, I say! Don't you have any pity at all for the old woman who's been good to you these many years?'' Sudden rage rose and spilled over. ''Drawing her into arguments—defying orders—''

Divino's eyes widened, then narrowed, then she leaped at me. I flung myself back, but even braced against the wall I had no defense against the suddenness of the attack and I reeled under it. Claws raked at my face, my eyes; but the swift lunge had cost Divino her footing on the crunching shards of china and she went down, cursing. The aura, the pulsing light, was backed into a corner. God in heaven, what was this? But the thing did not want *me*; it was helpless. The aura fluttered weakly over the woman's back, attaching itself again, and all at once grew brighter. It had to have a home!

I reached the door and yanked it open against the debris. I was sick of the woman and her doings. "Get up," I grated, "or I'll hoist you up by the hair! And if you value your life, get out of here—*now*!"

Snarling, Divino stumbled to her feet. I shoved her out and slammed the door even as a final mighty crash sounded within.

"I'll not forget—I still got a trick up my sleeve—"

I walked away. No, she wouldn't forget. Upon this last encounter rested the whole strength of my decision. If I needed any further convincing I had it now. *Go before something worse happened!*

I continued on up to my suite; there, I thought to bathe my face where the claws had struck, but there were no marks. Nothing at all! No pulsing, angry scratches from forehead to chin, no bloodied tracks; my face was as smooth as ever it had been, my cheeks unblemished. I stared at myself in the mirror, not believing the evidence of my own eyes. I looked around the room; no magic there. How had it happened? I turned away at last, washed my hands and smoothed my hair, then descended to Madame. There was something that couldn't wait, that had to be done, and done now.

CHAPTER 17

I remember that scene well; I think I shall never forget facing the old lady across the desk. She was smiling and waiting for what I had to say.

She chuckled. "Must be something momentous." I sat stiffly. "Paulette, what's wrong?"

"I'm leaving." I'd had all kinds of speeches prepared, but instead I simply blurted it out. "Leaving Crecy."

She didn't appear shocked, or even taken aback. I couldn't understand her calmness. I felt a sense of loss. She said slowly, "So you want to leave the Château."

"Yes," I said, "I think it's best that I do."

"Where will you go?"

"Back to Lowelton, I expect, back to my old job if they'll have me."

"I see." She was still calm, still unperturbed. Had she guessed it? Prepared herself? No, I thought, this was the way she really felt. Didn't she care at all? My sense of loss deepened but I mentally squared my shoulders. "Is this your own choice or is it for some other reason?"

"It's my own choice." What else could I say? That I can't live in the same house with Divino and you need her? No she'll stay, I'll go, and you two will work together harmoniously once more.

"I see," Madame said again. "Well, so be it, if that is your decision. My request, though, is that you stay until after the doll showing. And then there is the wedding. The tenants will be expecting you to be there.''

I agreed, and when I walked out it was with my head held high.

The display began with a lecture, clear and brief, to inform Madame's listeners of the origin of each doll and its costume; this one's costume came from Holland because of his Naval service to the Queen, that one's costume from Russia in recognition of aid to lepers in India, still another had a costume from Japan, an honor given by the Imperial Court to the master of a flagship who ran a blockade in wartime. The guests crowded around, scribbling notes on their little pads. There were *oh*'s and *ah*'s and much discussion of the beauty and value of the objects displayed—the color and shading or texture of costume, the hats, the jewels, and the headdresses, the shoes: I could not have imagined the talk could run on so long.

At teatime Jason came in, almost a welcome interruption. He glanced at me then at Madame, his gaze obscure. Madame was over near the display table set up for the dolls. She was in animated discussion, explaining some particular item of dress. "How is it going?" he asked presently under cover of the chatter.

"Very well. But Mrs. Cromwell is coming. More tea, Mrs. Cromwell?"

Mrs. Cromwell's white hair almost seemed to quiver with excitement; she had her Hector firmly in tow. Enthusiasm rose in intensity; one group drifted away to be replaced by another. Jason too drifted away; I didn't see him again until the party began to break up.

When I rose from my chair he was beside me. Most of the guests had gone; teacups and saucers made a clutter on the table, along with bits of cake, spilled milk. Someone had overturned a pitcher and used napkins to sop up the mess; they lay in a milk-soaked heap at a corner of the table. The dolls had been returned to the case and Madame was locking it preparatory to returning to her suite. The maids hurried to clear away the litter. There was to be a wedding tonight.

Leaving for Madame's office, we passed servants already coming to prepare the main salon for the ceremony. Maids carried potted plants, jardinieres of ferns, vases of flowers. A broad runner had been unrolled to form an aisle. Smiles, smiles and good cheer; all was lighthearted and pleasant. I wished I could lift my spirits accordingly. Yet wasn't everything settled? I'd made my announcement and it had been accepted—much too calmly and agreeably, I thought, then wondered if it wasn't my own unwillingness to do as I must, to face the fact of my self-imposed exile, that was part of my depression.

I looked at the old lady now and smiled. Presently Jason and I would leave and allow Madame to rest an hour before the evening's festivities commenced. A day like this was difficult and tiring, but I saw no weariness on her face at all.

I entered into the talk, but I was miserable. The easy acceptance of my announcement puzzled me. Did the old lady think so little of my work that it could be dispensed with so lightly, or even more important, think so little of the warm and wonderful relationship which had grown up between us that it could be tossed aside so casually? Despite all my rationalization, I felt lost and forlorn.

After I left Madame, I read in the lounge for a time, trying to settle my thoughts, then ascended to my suite and readied myself for the wedding.

Chairs had been carefully arranged and when I arrived the large room was already filled to capacity. I found a seat and someone played the wedding march. Jason appeared. "Here they come," he groaned.

"Yes." The petrified one, I knew, was the groom. Was he having second thoughts?

"Dearly beloved, we are gathered here together—"

As usual, Jason had seated himself near me. There were rows upon rows of chairs, just like in a church. I could believe the whole of Crecy was present, even poor Mrs. Edis, who evidently had enough chin-up determination to see the matter through. One old gentleman—I couldn't remember his name—slept peacefully, his white beard spread fanlike across his chest.

The room was breathtakingly beautiful. The profusion of flowers and ferns made it look like a woodland bower. The bride wore pink and she had feathers in her hair.

I had been sitting quietly staring at one spot before I realized I was looking at a figure posed casually against a bank of lilies and hydrangea. My eyes snapped shut then opened again; he was still there. A guest at the wedding? *But what kind of guest?* I was sure Jason didn't see him, nor Madame, nor any of the others.

I watched, fascinated. A big man, broad—? Then he turned. It was Thomas! One corner of his mouth lifted, the mustache twitching. As clear as day I saw his eyes roll heavenward and his hands clasp soulfully to his chest. I almost choked. His sword hung down, the tip nearly on the floor. It slowly lifted, pushed at Mrs. Cromwell's ample rear tonnage, and shied away again. I stared. The apparition wore high shining pirate's boots, the cuffs rakishly pulled down, and balloon trousers of velvet or some such material. A ring—the ring of opal and ruby I'd seen in the portrait—gleamed on his hand. A sardonic expression on his dark face, he looked directly across at me and winked.

The bride shivered suddenly, she glanced around then clung tight to Hector's arm. The latter stood, a bulwark of protection and completely oblivious, while the preacher droned on. The sword tip crept forward—I closed my eyes.

"What's the matter?"

"Nothing!" I whispered.

Jason's arm managed to crowd mine. "Then what were you staring at?"

I closed my lips tight and shook my head. Thomas was wandering among the flowers, flicking heads off nonchalantly here and there, but they didn't fall. The bouquets were all the same, roses, stephanotis, baby's breath, iris. There was the smell of wine in the air, wine and roses. In the front row in her wheelchair Madame sat solemn and regal. She didn't see any of it—didn't see Thomas at least. Where was Yvonne? I had come to wonder about that. The minister's

voice rose and fell monotonously, and at my elbow Jason
fidgeted. There was a stir at the back of the room and necks
craned. A maid slipped forward apologetically and leaned to
whisper to Madame, who turned and signaled to Jason.

Frowning, I looked after them as they left. So did other
people. I faced forward again to see the ceremony out,
wondering what was important enough to take the Mistress
of Crecy away from this momentous occasion.

It was over, the groom kissed the bride. Well-wishers
crowded around. Madame was gone and they were looking
to me. I was expected to officiate! I got to my feet and
plunged into the melee.

There was a reception, which the bride had requested.
Madame didn't return nor did Thomas, and for the latter I
was grateful. After the reception, the bride fluttered upstairs
to change then the couple followed their luggage to a
waiting coach amid a flurry of good wishes.

No one seemed to want dinner that night but it was served
anyway, at eight o'clock, which was an unholy hour for
Crecy tenants although most put in an appearance. Before
going to my suite, I descended to the dining room for coffee,
and became immediately engulfed in the backwash of the
wedding.

Didn't Mrs. Cromwell—Mrs. Brabington, rather—look
lovely? Almost radiant! They made a handsome couple.
Where did Mrs. Kirkwood say they were going? Oh yes,
Atlantic City. A honeymoon!

Was Madame Crecy well? She'd had to leave, someone
had given her a message. She was such a busy lady, with her
hands on the reins of this big house—

I managed to get away at last. Upstairs I reached for a
book, but couldn't read; unrest claimed me. Finally I laid
the book aside and once more sat by the window, looking
out. There was some malign infestation in the air; the house
and all around seemed to sit breathless, waiting. What did I
feel? I didn't know; I sensed a tragedy, perhaps, but tragedy
far off—not something destined for tonight. Tonight there
would be turmoil, storm. Leaves skittered across the yard

and the branches of the maples commenced to thrash; a fugitive moon made uncertain shadows across the lawn.

I thought of Albert, and how long I had waited. In the past weeks I'd tried to tell myself he might have moved to a different location where communication was more difficult; he might have had an accident—though I dared not dwell on such a possibility—or perhaps his orders had changed and he was on his way home. But I knew better. Such dreams were folly; there was no hope, I would never see him again.

Loneliness does strange things to people. When upon another night not long ago I'd stood before this same window and felt truly, in my heart, that he was gone, I'd even wondered what it would be like to be married to Jason. Would it be so bad? Loveless marriages were not unknown. But luckily I had suspected his duplicity, and now I shuddered to think that in one of my most desperate moments I could have given in to Jason's urgings.

Outside, the wind howled and raged and rain beat against the window, but inside, the room was still—too unearthly still.

I rose at last, disrobed and crept into bed, but moments later sat up, reached hurriedly for the bed lamp and switched it on. Yvonne stood with her back against the door. How silly to be alarmed! For I remembered I had something to say to Yvonne now, long held back.

"You finally came."

"I come where you are." Again the wrenching sadness; I had no patience with it.

"How can you bear to do the things you've done and still face me?"

"I?" The girl shook her head. "I have done nothing. You blame me for what happened?"

"Who else, then? You've played tricks before—"

"Jokes, never tricks. And those for but one reason. You think to run away, my Paulette? That will not be. You come from a long line of brave people, you can be brave, too."

"Brave?" I echoed bitterly. "Brave Uncle Simon hung himself—or would you know about that?"

"Ah, but that was foolish. Had he waited—"

"Had he waited . . . ?"

"Had he waited it would have gone away. Fine things were in store for him but he would not listen. He was headstrong! You see, there are some things we can help with, some we cannot."

I felt suddenly chastened, for what right had I to pillory this small shadow whose motives were so little understood?

"Trust me! This Thomas, he means no harm. He fools, he seeks fun, laughter, and games. I too sought laughter once, but I am serious now." She paused thoughtfully. "Though he does good, also. He sees in you an ally. Perhaps it is to make up for his bad ways before, I do not know. He too is serious at times. But not in the china closet. He was angry then. You did not see?"

"So it wasn't you?"

"No. It was Thomas."

"In the cellar?"

"Except for the lights, that was neither of us. It was the Evil."

"I see," I said on a long breath. "Why do you bring the scent of perfume with you?"

The slight wraith that was Yvonne shrugged, with a flash of whimsical humor and the old animation in her dark eyes. "It is your imagination. But the chill—you want to ask about that, as well? Is it not what is expected of us? It is not necessary otherwise, you know." She sank into a chair and stared at me. "I look long at you," she said, "for I shall not be with you much longer. Things will be—changed." She waved a hand. "Soon you will not see me anymore. I do not look ahead to that time." She added wistfully, "Has it been such a bad thing, then, that you should see us and talk to us? You are not the first, you know. Leonard was one."

"*The* Leonard? But I don't understand! They drove him out."

"He drove himself out. He felt an outcast—even as do you! Because he was different, they said, from the others. And so on down. There were others besides yourself. Many others. Is it such a shameful thing? We seek only to help and if our ways are not your ways it is because we are different from you. But I am glad of this time when there are no barriers between us. I will remember it and so, I think, will Thomas. That wild Thomas! We will be here, you will know; I am always near you, but for you I will be in darkness. You will inherit this castle and all in it, but we who helped you, you will not see us.''

I was first bewildered, then sharply impatient. I laughed mirthlessly. ''With all the problems here in this house? That I don't believe! As likely to see the stars change in their courses. What are you talking about? I don't—''

But Yvonne was suddenly nervous. She rose, and stood. ''Someone is coming,'' she said.

''I don't hear anything. Yvonne, wait—'' There was a knock on the door and I hurriedly got out of bed and reached for a robe. ''Just a minute—'' Yvonne was gone, and she had taken the scent of carnations with her. The *imagined* scent of carnations.

I opened the door to Doris, one of the new maids, and she extended a bulky envelope. ''Oh, mademoiselle, please— Madame said to deliver this long ago but I forgot. Divino gave me strict orders and there was so much work to do! I laid it down and—''

''Never mind.'' I smiled. ''It doesn't matter. We won't say anything about it. Thank you, Doris, and good night.''

''Thank you, mademoiselle—you are kind. I—Madame—I wouldn't want to get into trouble and I am new here. Thank you.''

I sat down with the envelope in my hands, thinking deeply. It was the craziest thing Yvonne ever said! Actually the whole conversation had been strange. What was I to believe of it? Nothing. Would Yvonne have Divino vanish in a puff of smoke? The differences in this household magically leveled? My own problem, of course, miraculously gone forever? Perhaps some of my remote ancestors had had the gift—I supposed that was entirely possible since it ran strong in the family. But Leonard surprised me; there were psychics in the Crecy family, too? More likely I had just misinterpreted.

I sighed and looked down at the envelope I held in my

hands. Was it the birthday gift Madame had promised? I broke the seal and the next moment stared in astonishment, for it was a document and, even at first glance, was recognizable as an itemized list of the dolls! And signed by Madame. It wasn't possible—what I was looking at couldn't be true. It was a deed conveying ownership of the Crecy collection of antique dolls to Paulette Kirkwood, free and clear, by reason of love and consideration.

I was stunned. Consideration of what? The love I knew. But why should Madame do a thing like this? The collection belonged to the family, had been in the family for generations. I couldn't accept it—it was not mine to take. I had no right.

My first impulse was to rush right down and protest but the old lady would be in bed by now. Later, much later, I went to bed too, but not to sleep.

CHAPTER 18

The gale had brought down branches and scattered the maple leaves upon the ground, and among them the sodden nest of baby robins lay cold and dead. I stood looking at the nest with pitying eyes.

"It tore the roses, too," old Noonan complained sorrowfully, for he had come to clear away the debris. "A bad summer storm. It were good we picked when we did. An' these little things—"

"I'll bury them," I said and bore the nest away. But I would try to take a lesson from the robins. The parents would not long forlornly grieve; they would pick up the threads of their lives and go on as Nature intended. Next spring they would forage for dried grass and twigs and build another home for a new batch of nestlings.

Sunday had dawned clear and fine. I had risen very early, breakfasted with Madame while the shredded gray clouds blew themselves out, and managed to thank the old lady with sincerity and affection for all her help and kindness.

The Manona doll had been returned properly repaired and the collection was again complete. Was there an air of finality about this, too? I was sitting in Madame's office, once again the tea things were spread upon the little table beside the desk.

"The present you gave me," I said, "is incredibly fine, but I have no right to it. No proper claim at all. The collection is yours; it belongs to your family. It is not mine."

"It is now."

"But why? I can't accept—"

"I asked that you not protest the gift, remember?"

I took a deep breath. I did remember. "I believe, though," I said quietly, "it's better if I leave it here, for the time being anyway. I'll have no place to keep it, and with something as valuable as that—"

"If you like," the old lady agreed pleasantly. "Whatever you choose to do with it, it's yours." Afterward, as though no change was contemplated, we chatted for a time of this and that, commonplace things, comfortable topics. The portrait had come back, she said, and was safely hanging in the gallery upstairs, all was complete at last and the room looked so much better.

"You've never seen the Manona picture, have you?" she asked. "A tremendous amount of dry rot was found in the frame, and the canvas seemed to be slightly damaged as well. I often wonder what pigments were used in that one, the surface seems so fragile. Or maybe it is the curse." She smiled. "Thomas swore it would fall apart, you know, an inglorious prediction. But the family was great for curses and predictions. In this enlightened age such things seem rather farfetched."

"Not too farfetched," I said carefully. "Though I suppose in a house as old as this one it is easier to believe."

"Ah, yes. It used to speak to me—fancies, of course. Even as a young widow I walked about half the time listening for things that weren't there." She paused. "I would like you to go upstairs and look at the portrait if you will, then come back and tell me what you saw."

It was like so many times before. I was pleased, but not too surprised, for she'd often asked my opinion on various matters, and I was glad, as always, to do her bidding.

The halls were quiet, peaceful. My bags were packed, except for what I needed for the night, and on the morrow, early, I would leave the Château forever. Therefore now, on my way to the gallery, I wandered slowly through the second floor, trying to take it in with new eyes, to store away each image and impression. There is where I'd met Albert; here, in this hallway, I'd crashed into Divino.

The manager, chastened, I supposed, by the last scolding from the old lady, was keeping out of sight. Just as well, I thought. Continuing on to the gallery, I turned inside.

It was as Madame said, the room was complete. Every space was filled and each frame gleamed with shining luster befitting its bright-plumaged occupant. Thomas was there, and beside him his famed Manona, all Polynesian in coloring; the eyes were pure Chinese—long, slanted, and enigmatic. But that face—slowly I froze; as I looked, the world tipped and fell away beneath my feet. This Manona—I was seeing myself—I was Manona. The face, the eyes, were my own, the hair. Only in the skin tone was there a slight difference, hers a little darker. My resemblance to Yvonne paled by comparison.

I found my throat dry and swallowed to relieve it. How could such a thing be? Manona—Thomas—these people were all Crecy in direct line. Yet there she was, offering nothing, revealing nothing—only myself. So great was the likeness that, save for dress, had she stood where I was standing now, and I in the frame, we could have been mistaken, one for the other.

No wonder Jason stared when first he saw me! Divino, and Madame; Divino with her hatreds already raging the minute I stepped into the house. My thoughts tumbled, I couldn't think straight. In a daze I turned and went out.

"Well," Madame said, "what did you think?"

"It seems to be a beautiful job of restoration," was all I could find to say.

"Sit down and let me tell you a story," she said, and after I was seated, continued. "You saw that cradle, wondered about Lionel. Thomas and Manona had four sons, Nathanaël Pierre, Léonard Gaston, Lionel Thomas, and Raoul Emile— Raoul named after a Spanish friend. Raoul died; Nathanaël fell in war; Lionel settled in France; after a family altercation Léonard left home never to be heard from again. It is said he went to America. There was that split in the family."

There had been a split in my family too, and far back in my memory a little bell rang. Was there something about a Raoul, and a Gaston—Leonard Gaston? My palms were wet; I sat awaiting her next words.

"You saw the Manona doll too, but that is no fair likeness. The portrait was from life. When I said you reminded me of someone, that is what I meant." She smiled and it lit up her face. "You can't leave, you know. I need you."

Madame kindly realized I needed time alone to think. I bid her good night and retired.

It was difficult to absorb what I'd heard and seen. What rang most strongly in my ears as I went over all she'd said, what sank deepest, was that the old lady needed me, wanted me. Many things stirred in my mind and came together. Her determination, by one means or another, to keep me here; the plunge into Château management, which would be my right, if I belonged. An heirloom gift worth a king's ransom, and the envy of kings. Then my name Iona, was it a derivation of Manona? And last but not least, I recalled what Yvonne had said, as if she knew something, or was certain of my position.

I looked at my bags, all packed and ready, and realized with wonder that I didn't have to go. What did it matter if it were really true I was family or not? My place was here.

I didn't know how Divino would take it, or Jason, but so far as the manager was concerned, some reasonable solution would have to be worked out. As for Jason, I hadn't seen him since the wedding. I'd grown so tired of his importunings; I'd planned on getting away before seeing him. Now—I didn't know.

Sleep eluded me, I was too full of the affairs of the day. Perhaps a walk—I rose at last and let myself out quietly. Since Madame's near accident from the loosened chock, I had checked them regularly and carefully, but how long did it take to loosen a chock? Whoever did it could try again.

I went downstairs and came, by force of habit, to the

ramp nearest her suite, her favorite and the one she always used when descending to the first floor and the gardens.

In deep shadow I knelt to explore the small protuberances nearest me—these, at least, were secure. Rising to change position to reach others, I was gripped sharply from behind by a pair of heavy arms, a big hand clamped over my mouth and nose. There was no air left to breath—I could not breathe!

I struggled frantically, twisting sideways to break that smothering hold, and the bulk that clutched me, was thrown off balance, stumbled, seemed to swing in the air then, with a wild yell, tumbled over and over all the way to the bottom, and lay still.

Voices broke out below; lights came on. I had only seconds to decide what to do. Swiftly I drew farther back into the shadows. It was Jason down there—dead, for no human body could be twisted so, and live. Madame cared about Jason, trusted him; if I told her what had happened, it would destroy her image of him.

There were empty apartments nearby; I stood behind a door, pushed hard against the wall so I could remain standing. I was trembling with shock in every limb.

Madame had burst from the office, calling loudly, "What is it? What's going on down there? Then, *"Oh, my heaven—!"* There was the wild jangle of the bellpull, more shouts, voices. "But he must have—" someone cried, and others called, "What happened?"

I could close my eyes, sick, and see that crumpled figure at the foot of the ramp. An odd taste was in my mouth, the taste of shock. He'd attacked me, tried to kill me, it was his intent to kill. They would think I didn't know anything about it, that up in my rooms on the third floor, I had slept through it all.

Long after the tumult died I crept quietly from my hiding place, and returned by the back way, to my quarters. A man walked this earth, laughed, talked, contrived, and the next moment he was dead. I didn't go to bed, I could not have slept anyway; I couldn't stop quaking inside.

In the final seconds of the struggle, iron fingers had

encircled my throat in one last vicious clutch. I wore a high-necked shirtwaist for the next few days to hide the bruises; the hoarseness of my voice I attributed to a slight cold.

The whole episode was a bad dream, a nightmare. Madame calmed the tenants; it was an accident, that was all they knew. Mr. Nettleton somehow caught his heel in the carpet and fell. He had been known to come late to see Madame upon some matter of business, but rarely this late. At any rate, he had cut across the top of a ramp and tripped on a chock. A tragic accident.

I imagined the talk went on endlessly, in the lounges, the dining room; little knots of tenants converging in small groups to discuss every detail. Madame went down and moved freely among them, calming, reassuring, and I marveled. No wonder they trusted and depended upon her as they did!

When she was able to return to her office, we sat together quietly. There was no urgent work, the house was silent. She had asked me specifically to be with her, and for a time, there seemed little to say.

She spoke at last. "He said he had something to talk to me about, but would be late. I told him to wait until morning. I wonder why he—" She shook her head and was again silent.

"It was—horrible," I said.

"Yes. I wouldn't have wanted it to happen like this."

I didn't know what to say. I didn't know what she meant. It was a strange remark. The death had been so sudden, Jason's attack so sudden and so violent, then he'd gone down in a great plunge. An inert figure at the bottom of a ramp.

"It is not an appropriate time, I know," Madame said, "but I'm going to be frank. Jason was not what he appeared to be. He had been siphoning off Crecy money for three years. The first year not much, the second he became bolder, and so on. He thought I didn't know, that I was charmed— mesmerized by his flamboyant personality—but that was not the case."

I heard, astonished. "Why didn't you put a stop to it if you knew?"

"I was curious—how far would he go? He had ingratiated himself into my affairs, my household, rising almost to the status of a son. Or so he thought. In the meantime he was doing good work for me—he was clever, and kept Château affairs in line. His own affairs he didn't manage so well." She paused again, then continued. "Most of his money was going toward the purchase of a building downtown. I own that building, so it's been funneling right back to me."

All this was hard to take in. That the old lady had the situation firmly in her grasp, was aware he was using her and was using him in return, astounded me. And even with this, I was glad I had said nothing about the attack. It wouldn't have changed anything, anyway.

"If you had shown real interest in him, I would have made a clean breast of the whole matter at once. What I had to give I gave long ago; my will had been changed to leave Hilda a comfortable annuity, but not the Château. She'll know this when she leaves. And this house would never have gone to Jason."

As for Hilda, she'd been deeply worried about her. She'd wanted to give Divino every chance after her many years of service. But the temper explosions and irascibility, the difficulties the manager had been causing, and above all, her offensive and disruptive dislike of me, could not be tolerated. For some time Madame had not known the extent of that dislike, but gradually she became aware of it. That was the end. She'd discharged Hilda, given her ten days' notice. I knew it must have greatly disturbed the old lady to sever a relationship of many years' standing, but she did not show it. Practical and direct as ever, once the decision was made, she carried it out without delay. She would shortly be interviewing replacements; there was a German woman with excellent qualifications. Château life must go on.

Yet I wondered, could she really get rid of Divino that easily? I doubted the woman would leave even if ordered to do so. Hilda Divino would be a wealthy woman anyway; it shouldn't matter to her where she lived. Like Jason, she had never cared for Crecy for its beauty, only for its value.

Then why did I feel the business with the manager was not finished? Why this terrible sense of fear, of darkness and dread? It seemed to hover over me, over all of us, like a thick cloud. The house had already seen death, what more could happen?

The manager was keeping out of my way—on purpose, I suspected, but she would be blaming me for her dismissal, letting it fester in her thoughts. Evidently her heavy hand was not being felt in the kitchens for there had been no more complaints. But was all as peaceful as it seemed on the surface?

The next afternoon a Mr. Peters, Solicitor, was announced.

Madame looked up from her papers at once. "Jason's partner? I wonder what he wants?"

"Should I go?" I asked, thinking it might be something the old lady would prefer dealing with in private.

"No, stay," she said, "there is no reason why you shouldn't." I'd noticed a new freedom in her; she was far less watchful and tense. It was as though she had come to terms with something in her mind.

Mr. Peters was ushered in, a small, stooped individual in pince-nez and a conservative gray-striped cutaway.

"Mr. Peters?"

"Madame Crecy. I am delighted." The freshness of Ireland was in his speech. He placed a briefcase carefully beside his chair before seating himself. Obviously a man of directness, he got to the point at once, but only after noting my presence and looking me over rather thoroughly.

"Actually it is Miss Kirkwood I came to see." He peered at me over his glasses. "You are Miss Kirkwood, are you not?"

"Yes."

"Um, yes, of course. It is my duty to inquire. It seems there has been a gross miscarriage of all that is decent and proper. I refer to Mr. Nettleton—no offense meant, you understand, but the truth is always best. Well, suffice it to say that the late Mr. Nettleton was guilty of theft. He had been thieving letters.''

"Letters!'' I sat up straighter.

"Aye, letters. How or when he managed to obtain them I do not know, but I do know where they were secreted. I only found them today, hidden well down in the bottom of a cabinet in his office. I am contemplating expansion and, as a necessity, his material must be cleared out, boxed and stored, or in a case such as this, returned to the rightful owner.''

I had been sitting on the edge of my chair. Now Mr. Peters rose, opened his briefcase, and with a polite bow to Madame who was also impatiently waiting, dropped a pile of letters—at least a dozen of them—on the desk before us.

They were all addressed to me. Albert! My heart started to beat in an odd, muffled sort of way. Letters from Albert—Jason had taken them—*stolen* them, and hidden them away where they could not be found! Those times when he came to collect the post, his regular early visits to Crecy—he must have taken them then.

"My—word,'' Madame murmured.

It was hard for me to speak. And all this time I'd thought Albert hadn't written, that he'd not cared enough to even send a brief few lines! Tears were close, and I blinked them back.

"I believe these are yours.'' Madame gathered up the envelopes and handed them to me with an understanding smile. She'd liked Albert, had asked about him; her failure to do so these past few weeks had told me of her sympathy and continued support.

Solicitor Peters cleared his throat. "I appear to be the bearer of exceedingly bad tidings—or good tidings, as you will, seeing that justice must be done. As you know, the gentleman of whom we speak was once married. The unfortunate girl fell to her death down a flight of stairs; the child she was to bear perished also. One views such tragedies with the greatest sorrow for the bereaved; everyone did in this instance. However, I shall be quite frank to say that such sorrow was misdirected. The case has been reopened—actually it was never closed—with the result that fresh evidence has been uncovered. It is almost certain that Mrs. Nettleton's death was not accidental. She was murdered.''

''Murdered!'' Madame echoed.

''It is believed so, yes. Mrs. Nettleton's parents, the Peter Dowlings of this city, have been most tireless in pressing the issue. The Dowlings are quite wealthy, and have left no stone unturned in the furthering of the investigation, bringing it to a satisfactory conclusion. Their daughter's murderer would have been brought to the dock. From the start, they strongly opposed the marriage and blocked inheritance of any kind by Mr. Nettleton, through his wife.''

Part of this I already knew. Madame had told me some, but I was appalled to realize how I had been taken in.

''Well—'' Mr. Peters got to his feet and picked up his briefcase. ''I wish my visit had been a more pleasant one,''—he smiled slightly—''but perhaps my ill tidings are somewhat balanced by the restoration to this young person of what is rightfully hers.'' He nodded gallantly; the Irish came out in the lively twinkle of his eyes. ''Good day to you, ladies.''

Madame rang and a maid came to show him out. ''That was nice of Mr. Peters,'' I said, for I hadn't forgotten my thanks.

''Very nice,'' murmured the old lady. ''I am so glad, and so grateful. The sun will shine for you now.''

''Oh, I hope so,'' I said, ''I do hope so!''

CHAPTER 19

Albert had been sick, the second letter said, deathly ill with fever, and was only now recovering. It was going slowly, but it would not be long until he was on his feet again. I wept over those pages. He wondered why I hadn't written, waited for word that didn't come.

I think back to the time we were together, he wrote, *and remembered what I said, but there was so much more I had wanted to say. To tell you again how I regret the shameful way I treated you in my foolish youth, but mostly to explain what I found when my vision cleared. I would not dare speak as I do if I were not sure that what I saw in your face and in your eyes that day was true. It will bring me back. I am counting the hours.*

Another letter was informative and cheerful, but I read discouragement in every word. Still another almost desperately questioned why I hadn't answered, and still another, the last and dated the most recently, stated that he couldn't understand my silence—there must be some reason. Because of his illness he would be leaving soon, and would come directly to the Château. He hoped I'd still be there. Love breathed through every page, and I touched them longingly.

Jason could have burned these precious missives! I shuddered to think of it. Each envelope bore a return address but it was too late now to reply; before I could get word to him he would be on his way home.

Madame was shocked at what had happened. She had suspected Jason of many things, but not of the pettiness of stealing letters. Yet in this the motive was clear; I was to believe Albert had abandoned me. Beyond that, he meant to wear me down to the point where I would eventually accept his proposal of marriage.

If I proved to be a member of the Crecy family or otherwise in line for inheritance, it would come to him, through me. My end, no doubt, was to be the same as that of his first wife. But because I continued adamantly to refuse him, he tried to kill me.

Were his continued efforts to bring about Divino's expulsion from the Château, even when he suspected I had supplanted her in Madame's affections, prompted only by resentment? Or by determination to keep the manager from realizing anything at all from the estate? There would always be unanswered questions. Aware of his under-handed activities, Madame had quietly moved ahead to what she wanted to do.

The old lady was of course aware of his attacks against Divino—ostensibly for the old lady's own good—in general, she dismissed the dissension between Jason and the manager as a personality clash. Few were able to get along with Hilda Divino.

Later that same afternoon Madame suggested tea in the garden.

"Now?" I echoed. I don't like ramps, I was about to say.

"Yes. Why not? The weather is lovely, and it will be good to get out." And when I still hesitated, she added, "Come now. It's all right. I've not been there for some time though I used to go very often."

So short a while ago there had been a terrible accident on that same ramp—now she wanted to go down it, in the wheelchair? Though the chocks were safe, for I had personally inspected them just this morning, I shrank from the descent. If there was only some other means of reaching the garden!

"Do you think it's wise?" I asked.

"There has been a death," she said gently. "Nothing like it has happened before. What better reassurance than for them to see me do what I have always done?"

She was right and I couldn't argue with her, no matter how I felt.

"I love my garden. It was begun in my girlhood. I was barely eighteen when I came here, so you see I had a hand in its inception. My father insisted upon adding the flower-pots; they were terrible, huge gaudy things of weird shapes. We got rid of them as soon as we could. Gave them to a traveling peddler, as I recall. My father never went there so it didn't matter anyway. So far as he was concerned I should have dumped the whole place and gone back to France."

"Is his portrait upstairs?"

"Oh yes. On the far wall, the portly, somewhat pompous gentleman with the long mustaches. He favored hair and a lot of it, said it gave a man dignity."

I wheeled her carefully, listening to her talk. I thought she was putting herself out to be entertaining and any other time I would have enjoyed it. What was wrong with me? The chocks were in perfect condition and this was only a pleasant afternoon's excursion. The tea things were already in the garden on the little wrought-iron table—the teapot in its cozy to keep the contents hot against the outside air, the sugar and creamer, the dainty cups and napkins. I spied Dulcey hurrying with a covered dish of scones, which would still be warm from the oven. There was someone else too, paused in the doorway. She glanced up to check our progress. Shock hit me; Divino! The way she was standing, the way the light struck her features, her face was a dark mask.

I was finding it difficult to keep my thoughts on what Madame was saying. When I came to the top of the ramp I hesitated.

Madame still chattered cheerfully. "I've always been thankful I put in these ramps; I could scarcely have gotten around otherwise, with so many sets of stairs in the house, yet I think they have served their purpose. Next month I am installing elevators throughout.''

The part about the elevators registered, all the rest was just words. To fill up space? I was moving forward in a vacuum, we were enclosed in a cocoon together, what was going to happen would happen and there was no way to stop it. My vocal chords were locked, I couldn't speak.

Was there a Presence beside me? A bulk which paced behind me, whose footsteps I heard, but whose image I could not see? A hand on the wheelchair beside my own.

The old lady was speaking of a begonia, of a special shade she liked. In past years she had planted them herself. She wanted me to take particular note of the color. Divino was now at the foot of the ramp, staring upward, still watching our progress. Could I be wrong; was she there to help after the descent was made? Then all my thoughts fled, for I was pulling back hard on the heavy chair; It was going too fast down the incline, I couldn't halt its too rapid movement. I couldn't control it anymore—Madame was clutching for support to save herself.

"Paulette!" she shouted. "The brake—the brake!" sobbing, I cried back, "There is no brake—it's gone—it doesn't—work! Madame—*Madame*!" Then suddenly we were falling, there was nothing to hold on to. In a blur I saw Hilda Divino's face, bloated, purple, heard the rage that spilled from her. "—Not going to cheat me—Twenty years—"

The chair would hit her—why didn't she move out of the way? We were going to crash—

The chair tipped; at the last moment I threw myself before Madame, before the wheelchair to stop its flight with my own body; the earth spun then splintered into a million brilliant, exploding stars. I was dimly conscious of a great weight atop me, pressing me down, crushing out my breath and breaking my bones.

"Help, help!" I screamed though it was only a thread of sound in my throat. "I have killed *Maman*—" Then something hit me with terrific force and I knew nothing more.

There was a body falling. It could see and hear but had no substance and no volition of its own. Sun, moon, and stars rocketed in a gigantic swirl, they wouldn't stop, and little pinpoints of light broke off and fell gentle, like rain. Everything was gentle here, no hurry, but I was not a part of it, not yet.

I felt a weight pressing against me and pushing me down so I could not breathe and I struggled against it. I was one with the earth and felt damp in all my members. It was on my hands and could not be shaken off. The great weight pressed until all breath was gone and I was one with the falling stars and the moon and the whirling voices. Then suddenly and miraculously the crushing weight lifted and I was free.

There were words coming at me from somewhere, a soft, gentle babble of many voices speaking together, a hum and buzz of talk, but I was still not a part of it. Words were released from my mind and trying to join the others. I could feel them but my lips did not move. They were rising out of my mind and were all around me.

Why was I swimming in a stream? It went against me. Someone was angry, someone was calling, was it the same voice? No, only an obstruction in the stream, and I had to go around it and that made me angry—the rushing sound was too great and I couldn't hear what I was suppose to hear. Now the voice was insistent. Why couldn't they understand? I could hear it, plainly.

I walked somewhere in a valley, Thomas walked beside me, he kept telling me to be careful and not to fall. How could I fall with him holding my arm? I told him how foolish it was, doing what he did. But it was too late. All that had come and gone and now it was my turn. But they wouldn't let me pass! I'd told Yvonne to meet me here. Who was Yvonne? I didn't quite remember Yvonne— someone I was suppose to know.

Why couldn't they be quiet and go away, those voices? They needled at me, kept picking at my hands, my face, one of them put cold pressure on my head. I was falling—no, I wouldn't fall, ever again. I didn't have to be afraid anymore.

"Take it easy, take it slow and easy," Thomas said. His face was in shadow but I knew he was smiling. He was kind! "Slow—and—easy. Step down or you will fall."

"I won't fall. Because I'll never fall again. Not ever! I'm not afraid."

"No, you don't understand. I cannot be around to help you. You will have to go by yourself. Will you listen to me? You have to know that I will not be with you to help you. None of us will."

"But where am I going?" There was fear in my voice, near panic. "Where am I going? I don't understand!"

"You must listen! I tried to tell you. All this is for you but you must do it alone. No one can do it for you. We have come as far as we can but can go no farther. It is like a great forest you must pass through and there will be light on the other side. All good! Can you believe me?"

"I believe—" Thomas was holding me but his touch slipped away. I felt his touch slipping away from me. But where was Thomas? He had gone. I stood alone in the darkness and the wind blew cold against my body. I was alone and no one could go through this passage but myself. I felt the words come; I called but there was no answer.

"They don't want me, either."

And then someone from the other side: "Who doesn't want you?"

"Why, Yvonne and all the rest," I said impatiently. "They say I can't stay. Why couldn't they understand, why did they have to be so obtuse? You don't know it's like this. It's not like you think at all. It's dark over there. At first it's dark. After that it gets light and the light is everywhere you are. Wherever you go. You bring the light with you. Because you think it is supposed to be daylight, it is daylight. You can wish the sunshine, too. Why wouldn't they let me stay?" My voice sounded plaintive and I grew impatient again and with the impatience came restlessness. It wasn't working out right at all, it wasn't supposed to be like this. Why did they keep picking at me? I wished they would go away!

"Why don't you go away?" I said and tried to push them

aside, but there were a thousand fingers, all pulling and tugging at me. It had taken so long to get this far!

The trees were thick and green; there was a pool, and fish swam in it. There was a pink flower in a green pot beside the pool, a favorite pink flower, and someone had placed a teapot and cups on a table. What was a table doing here? There was no one to use it, no one to drink the tea or to watch the birds bathing in the pool. But the birds were dead! No, not all of them, only the little ones. There were leaves everywhere, and branches, and I shivered in the wind. Yvonne shouldn't let them do this to me!

"Yvonne!" I cried but Yvonne didn't answer. She had gone, too. "I think they must all lack perception," I said. The warmth was with me once again, for I sat with Nathaniel in the shadowed dusk and spoke, laughing, of many things. But it was not Nathaniel! Who was it, then? I stared up at the man with me and the whispering began once more. There were faces and those hands. I pushed the hands away.

"How far have I been?" I asked.

"Not far."

So now the voices were answering! I had no desire to leave and therefore cast about for what I must say. But thoughts skipped ahead, tantalizing and just out of reach.

"I don't believe you. I've traveled for weeks. I've been there—and back."

"Where? Where have you been?"

It was no use. They were so stupid. They would never understand. I would be sly—I wouldn't tell them, then. It was the only thing that made me different and if I didn't tell them they wouldn't know, would they?

"She's coming around," somebody said with relief. "She'll be all right now."

"I'm tired," I muttered.

"Of course. Just lie still."

"No. Tired of lying here." And suddenly my eyes snapped open. It was daylight, the sun was shining and memory rushed back. *"Maman!"* I screamed and struggled with the coverlet for I was in bed and someone was watching over me.

"All right. It's all right! Just lie quietly now."

It was a stranger, the face bearded, the eyes bright blue. At first I saw nothing beyond my range of vision, only the fat little man. My head felt light and I touched it, and my hair. My eyes felt strange too, hard to focus, as if they had been closed for a long while. The little man rose; he snapped his bag shut and set it on the table.

"I want to get up."

Then I saw Madame by the other side of the bed. I frowned, puzzled. But Madame—and the wheelchair—

She pushed herself close and touched my cheek with gentle fingers, then took my hand in a hard, firm grip that almost hurt. "You've been wandering," she said and her voice was not steady. "Thank God you're back! I couldn't understand why you were out so long. Or how it happened you weren't hurt badly, even killed, instead of bruised and shaken up. You threw yourself in front of the wheelchair to stop it—the brake was gone."

"You weren't injured?"

"Only a bumped ankle."

The doctor nodded briskly. "I've already told you what to do," he said to Madame, "keep your foot elevated. I know your impatience, but see that you obey my orders. This young lady here is to remain in bed for at least two days. Other than bruises she's as sound as a dollar. A fine healthy specimen, I'd say. Well, I'll look in on you again in a day or so." He picked up his hat and bag and went out.

I pulled myself up carefully against the pillows. My body felt battered and I was sore in every joint but my mind felt wonderfully clear and sound.

"I thought," I said, "that we were going all the way to the bottom. Did we—did the chair hit Mrs. Divino? She was standing there; we must have struck her unless she moved aside at the last minute. How is she? Is she hurt?"

A cloud passed over the old lady's face. "She got her coat, her valises, walked to the front porch, down the steps, and fell dead of apoplexy."

Shock held me silent. Finally I asked, "Did she—?"

"Render the brake useless? Yes. She knew better than to meddle with the chocks, they were too well patrolled, but the brake line was deliberately cut. She had hate in her and it had to come out. In the end it killed her. The tenants knew she was leaving, and believe she left, but that's all they do know." Madame paused. "I sat here and listened," she said. "You talked to Thomas, and spoke of Yvonne, and of Nathaniel."

It was very quiet in the room. A bee buzzed past the open window and down in the garden a bird raised his voice in a sudden burst of song. We were in the quarters beyond Madame's office, and my cot had been pushed up before the window. The wheelchair was close beside me.

"Yes," I said. "I see and hear things other people can't hear and see. Yvonne Spieret, Thomas, others. They are all over on the other side—the old part. Thomas was at the wedding." I took a deep breath. Now I'd started I couldn't stop. Madame sat quietly, head bent, listening.

"It was Yvonne in the hall; she was as real as you or I. She's come to me in the halls, in my suite. I've talked with them countless times. It was Yvonne who tampered with the lights. She said the house needed shaking up, things weren't happening fast enough. Thomas blocked work in the Old Wing. He let the carpenters see him; that's why they quit. The old section is what they know, they are at home there. To Thomas, Crecy is still his. He resented the reconstruction, the tearing down, as he termed it. I think he understands now though and if you were to begin work again he wouldn't interfere. I was led here. You know that little street below the house, at the bottom of the hill? Limpole Road. I saw what life was like, back then! I was almost run over there by a dray. You think I'm crazy but I'm not. I've been this way all my life, my curse since I was born, always funny, never like other people, that's why I was afraid to let anybody in."

The old lady looked up. "This convinces me more than any one thing, that you are of Crecy blood. My husband lost his second sight when we were married. My dear, why

didn't you tell me! I was waiting for proof. Forgive a
stiff-necked old woman, I have all the proof I want. If legal
proof comes tomorrow, next week, next year, or never, it's
all the same. I'm glad you told me but it doesn't matter how
you got here or what went before. You're here, and you are
family.''

Had the hand on the wheelchair been Thomas's? Who
could explain, within the bounds of cool-headed logic, such
a journey as I had taken? To human experience it was a
borderline dream, nothing more; I knew better.

Never had the house seemed so peaceful or so pleasant.
A little maid hummed as she wheeled a tea cart down the
hall. It was Janette, the girl who had so sunnily wished
Madame happiness as she bore away the box of tissue
wrappings at the conclusion of the birthday celebration.

I had much to look forward to and much to accomplish.
There was the long-delayed cataloguing of the doll collection; I'd promised to do that. Always I was alert to Albert's
arrival.

I was at work in the Trophy Room, facing the door, when
I looked up and saw him. I never remembered crossing the
room; the next moment we were in each other's arms. He
was thin, so thin! But his dear face mirrored all I had hoped
to see. His lips were on mine, and again, and again,
hungrily, my tears on his cheek.

No words were spoken, none were needed. I had come
home, and Albert had come home.

EPILOGUE

So this was the way it happened. They brought me here for a purpose and I hadn't believed. I would have liked to thank those Silent Ones, but they are gone. Forever. They would be around as before, but not for me.

The tenants were deeply shocked at Jason's death, but they thought, as Madame said, that the *directrice* had simply left Crecy's employ. It was just as well; this loyal group had weathered enough storm.

We never knew whether or not Jason was to blame for the loosened chock, and Hilda Divino is past answering. I was certain my suspicions were correct; that she had placed the tainted water glass on my table as harassment, hoping it would frighten me into leaving, set the fire in the closet and tampered with the heater for the same reason.

When Jason came to Crecy he was aware that Divino was to inherit, and began his campaign against her. Then I appeared, a far greater threat than ever Divino had been, for he recognized me at once. Marriage, to me, was his goal, failing that, he'd grown desperate. The near tumble that day in the Old Wing was no accident; I'd been pushed. Rage and frustration must have overtaken him when he found me at the top of the ramp. How he expected to get away with what he had in mind I don't know; greed makes strange decisions.

I only know, looking back upon it, that we have come through deep waters, have earned our freedom and are content. And yes, *Maman* is still with us, a bit slower perhaps but she retains a voice in Château affairs. Mostly these days she spends her time telling stories to two-year-old twins, who climb upon her knees and call her *Grandmère*—Grandmother.

If our children have second sight, we—Albert and I—have agreed to bring it out into the open and to help them deal with it, so they can regard it, not as something shameful, but as a condition to be lived with and understood. We may not succeed completely, but we can try.

Albert resigned from the Diplomatic Service; he says helping run Crecy is a full-time job.